MW00442430

THE
NEXT 60
OR SO YEARS

AIMEE DANROTH

WRITERS REPUBLIC L.L.C.
515 Summit Ave. Unit R1
Union City, NJ 07087, USA

Website: *www.writersrepublic.com*
Hotline: *1-877-656-6838*
Email: *info@writersrepublic.com*

Ordering Information:
Quantity sales. Special discounts are available on quantity purchases by corporations, associations, and others. For details, contact the publisher at the address above.

Library of Congress Control Number: 2021931920
ISBN-13:   978-1-63728-193-2   [Paperback Edition]
                978-1-63728-194-9   [Digital Edition]

Rev. date: 02/19/2021

To my best friend and cousin, Delaney. Thank you for always being my rock.

Kaylie, thank you for being the very first person to ever believe in my writing. I miss you every single day.

Chapter 1

"Why are we going to university just to drown in debt? We are going to be working as bartenders for the rest of our lives, I hope you guys know that." Farah blew the loose black strands away from her face, dropping the textbooks on the table were her tray should have been.

"Maybe we'll get lucky and beat the odds." Penny looked up at Farah, giving her a reassuring smile. Her dirty-blond hair was pulled up in a messy bun, and any attempt of makeup had worn off, showing her blemished skin.

Lucas picked around with his fork in the limp vegetables, scrunching his nose, making the thick black frames of his glasses rub against his eyebrows. "I understand why you are a vegetarian."

Farah stood staring at the steaming tray of food on the four of her friends' trays. Brooke, Penny, and Lucas were all trying to imagine the food was something else. Farah didn't even have to look up to know that Thomas had girls hanging off him.

"Okay, okay, ladies, I'm trying to eat," Thomas said with an exhausted tone.

Somewhere between his perfect white teeth, his tattoos, bulging muscles, daily gelled hair, girls didn't mind being turned down by him. He was captivating. The first day of classes last year Lucas randomly brought him to lunch, Penny, Brooke and Farah all became speechless at the sight of him. Penny was the first girl to sleep with him, but thankfully, both of them are mature enough; now they just pretend it never happened. Brooke slept with him a week later; she would do anything for it to happen again.

She has been head over heels for him since. He hasn't tried with Farah, and she's okay with that. He has made his way around the coeds once or twice.

"Farah."

Farah turned around to see Brett standing behind her with his hands in his jean pockets.

"I was wondering if you wanted to go for dinner with me tonight?"

Farah sucked in air between her teeth. "I'm sorry, I work tonight. Someone has to serve the alcohol."

Brett looked down at the ground and nodded.

She hated turning people down.

Farah pulled out a chair, listening to Penny loudly whisper, "That's the fifth date she shot down this week."

All four of her friends cranked their heads, looking at Farah. Her getting asked out on dates wasn't anything new. She never thought she was that attractive, but everyone around her knew she was absolutely stunning—her big emerald-green eyes, long pin-straight black hair, fake sun-kissed skin, defined cheekbones.

"What?"

Lucas put his elbow on the table, pointing at Farah. "You know every guy in school has a crush on you."

Thomas laughed, leaning into his seat, pushing the tray away. "She doesn't date. Everyone knows it. The only people who ask her are asking to be shot down."

"Just once, I want a date, just one damn date." Penny sighed.

Brooke grabbed Penny's shoulder. "Wednesday is Valentine's Day. Let's go out for dinner and cry into our wine."

Penny's eye light up as she turned her head toward Brooke, smiling.

Farah cringed. Valentine's day was nothing but a Hallmark holiday; all it does is makes people feel like shit because they were single. She made sure she was working that night. As much as she hated to admit it, she would love it if she had a guy to make a fuss about it just once.

"I'm going home to study." Farah grabbed her textbooks, standing up.

"I said a bad word," Brooke mumbled.

"Why are you even worried about school? You have your heart set on the military," Lucas said, deadpanned.

Ignoring him, Farah walked out of the cafeteria, plowing through the obnoxious football players, only to walk outside and be hit with the crowd of smokers standing out front. She briskly walked to the car, regretting her thin sweater. The February air in Las Vegas was brisk.

She unlocked the car, turned the key, and listened to the squeal, praying that her starter won't fail her again. Being a university student with a car had enough expenses. Farah pet the dash when the car started, cranking the heat. Growing up in Montana, she forgot what cold weather actually was. Living in the dessert for four years was long enough to get used to the dry weather.

Farah's older sister, Braelynn, bought a condo before she moved into her boyfriend's house. When she wasn't on tour, she stayed with him at his house. Farah, Brooke, and Penny moved into her vacant three-bedroom fully furnished condo, only paying the mortgage price. Braelynn hated what the condo originally looked like. The old owners had tacky orange carpet, and the cupboards were falling off the hinges. It looked like it was a crack house. Now, you would never suspect it. The floors were hardwood, the cupboards and the new appliances in the kitchen were black with white floor tiles. The only thing that was original were the big open windows looking down on Las Vegas.

The University, the condo, and the bar that all five of them work at were far away from the Strip. Any local wouldn't go near the Strip unless they felt brave enough. That far back from the tourist attractions, the city slept at night and the sidewalks were not full of entertainers begging for money. The city was almost normal.

Farah sat on the fake leather couch trying to comprehend what she learned in class that morning. Nothing could help her with history. Remembering dates was equally as hard as leaning a math equation. How she was even able to graduate high school, then get into university made no sense to her; she hardly had the grades to be accepted.

Farah read the same few pages, taking notes, retaking notes until the lock on the door clicked. She closed her books and looked down at her notebook. She saw a single tearstain. That only made her more frustrated. She wiped her face, grabbed the paper and textbooks, and stood up to toss them on her bed.

*****

"Why do we have to work at the college bar our classmates go to?" Penny shrieked over the drink orders.

Farah splashed Coke on top of a paralyzer, handing it to a girl from her English class. Beer orders, drink orders, and drunk college kids—all nudging them to move faster. Farah cracked open a Corona, dropped a lime in, and slammed it on top of the bar, shoving it to the douchebag quarterback. She flashed him the fakest smile she could muster and took the bill out of his hand, stuffing it in her billfold.

The bar finally cleared, and Thomas put his hand on the arch of Farah's back, pulling her into his body. He did this in the privacy in the apartment, but in public, her body tensed. She stepped away to look in his dark-brown eyes.

4

"If you touch me like that people are going to think we are sleeping together."

"Is that really a bad thing?" Thomas lips went in a half smile.

Farah laughed, opening another beer bottle. "I'm the only girl on campus you haven't made a move on. I think that says it all."

Thomas stood close to Farah, talking in her ear. "Wait, you want me to?"

Farah shook her head. "Definitely not."

"It hasn't been the entire campus. Get your facts straight."

Farah pulled away from Thomas, completely revolted. She looked over her left shoulder watching Brooke start to fume with anger. Farah rolled her eyes and continued to work, keeping up with the new crowd.

Even as Farah worked, she could feel Brooke's eyes on her. It wasn't just Farah; Penny and Lucas were fed up with her obsession with Thomas. Even Thomas was tired of it.

Brett stood in front of Farah, buttoned-up shirt with the sleeves rolled halfway up his forearm. His hazel eyes, dark hair, and olive skin made him a lot easier to look at—and a lot harder to turn down.

"I just wanted to see if you actually had to work or if you just hated me."

"Ha! I'm always working. What do you want to drink?" Farah leaned into the bar.

"Corona."

Farah put the beer on the bar for him to grab it.

"Everyone on the basketball team thought I was crazy since the only word you know is *no*. Just know I'm not giving up." Brett walked away, leaving Farah confused behind the bar.

"Now, he's more your speed," Brooke mumbled.

Farah slammed the cooler door, walking away. If she could get Brooke's mind from Thomas, all of their lives would be back to normal and finally back to a normal friend group. It was over a year ago since they spent one night together; she still won't drop it. If anything, she looked pathetic. Any girl who ends up getting feelings for Thomas was pathetic.

Chapter 2

All weekend Farah spent working, sleeping, and eating. Trying to come up with any time to study became a struggle a year ago. Every Monday and Tuesday she had to stay up as late as she could to try and finish the assignments that she never had time to do. Part of the reason it was so hard for her to concentrate was because of the voice in her head telling her how much of a disappointment she was. Her family paved a pathway for her two older brothers and older sister. As the golden children, the three of them went with their paths with no argument. Farah, on the other hand, had to apply for college behind everyone's back. No one other than her siblings even asked her what she was getting a degree in.

"You will join the military." Farah's parents made that clear since day one.

She was the odd man out in the family. She understood why it was important to them. That never changed the fact she was terrified. In six months, she would be twenty-three, the same age her oldest brother was when he was killed in battle. She refused to let that be her. No matter the damage it would cause.

Farah stood up, walked over to her dresser, and opened the drawer. Lying on top of her folded shirts was the application. Her father, the corporal, already signed the paper. She picked it up and ripped it. The sound of ripping paper never sounded so sweet. She put the paper together and ripped the two pieces into four, dropping it on the pile of textbooks.

"How did it take me twenty-two years to stand up for myself?" Farah lay in bed, shoving her textbooks over.

No more looks of admiration when people find out. Now when people see her, it's only going to be her they see. No obligation, no responsibility, just a struggling university student.

*****

"Wakey, wakey, eggs and backey!" Penny shouted as she made an entrance into Farah's room, shutting the door behind her.

Farah grunted. It felt like she had just fallen asleep. "Did you cook breakfast?"

"You know it. Eggs, toast, and fruit for my little vegetarian. Brooke is pigging out with Thomas and Lucas."

Farah got out of bed and walked over to her closet, picking up a bra off the floor, turning her back away from Penny. "How's Brooke's obsession this morning?"

"We both got asked out for tomorrow night. Hopefully that will help."

Farah spun around with her mouth opened. "Who?"

"Mike asked me, and Rob asked Brooke."

Farah ran over the guys in school with the same names, trying to pinpoint who was who. Two Mikes from the basketball team came to mind, but Penny would never be stupid enough to go out with one of them.

"More basketball players? What is with these guys?"

Penny shrugged with a smile. She was happy just to have a date. "Are you sure you want to go out there looking like that?"

"Mike Adkins, right?" Farah slipped the tank top over her head, waiting for Penny to nod. "Good, and if he hasn't tried to sleep with me, he never will." Farah looked down at her tight tank top and spandex shorts.

"Do I sense you are a bit upset about that?"

Farah shook her head, opening her bedroom door. She wasn't going to admit it to herself, but not having Thomas even try to make a move on her and having her set in friend zone before he even sat down at the table put a bit of a dent on her self-esteem.

A plate was already set out for Farah at the island. The sight of food made her stomach growl. She looked at Brooke. "I hear you have a date for tomorrow?"

Brooke stared at her plate. "Yeah. I don't know, he's not—"

"Just shut up." Farah cut Brooke off. She pushed out her chair looking at her. "Good God. Just stop."

Farah stormed off into the bedroom, suddenly not hungry anymore. As brutal as that was, someone had to tell her. The truth always hurts.

Farah put on jeans and a sweater over her tank top. She ran a brush through her hair and put on her makeup. Even with Farah's natural beauty, she wore enough just to highlight her features, plus layers on mascara to make her eyes pop. While she was putting on her red lipstick, the bedroom door opened.

"Thank you." Thomas shut the door, falling onto the bed. His sweater pulled up, revealing the tattoos peeking out of his sleeves. They were best friends, but oddly enough, they have never been alone before. "Up all night studying again?"

"Can't you tell from the bags under my eyes?" Farah sat down on the bed, lying next to him.

Thomas body went stiff when Farah hit the mattress beside him. She scrambled to her feet, turning around to face the closet. She held her hands and rested them under her chin. She took a deep breath, trying to figure out why he was so repulsed by her. If he won't even be three feet near her, she must be uglier then she thought. Farah knew it was insane to let a guy be the reason why you suffer from low self-esteem, but he made it pretty clear something was wrong with her.

"We need to go. We are going to be late for English." Farah walked around the bed, picking up the textbooks that she needed.

"What is this?" Thomas reached for one piece of ripped paper, then another. "This is your application. It's the application. Isn't this your dream?"

"It's my parents' dream. The military was never my plan."

Thomas looked at Farah wide-eyed.

"Hopefully, they won't be too mad. I'll only be a handful of Whitmores not to join."

"So, what you are saying is, I don't need to spend months on end worrying about you?"

Farah nodded hesitantly.

"Thank Jesus."

The relief in Thomas voice took Farah off guard. "Looks like we both are going to have a degree in humanities and won't know what to do with it."

*****

Farah, Tomas, and Lucas served two crowds of people at the bar that Valentine's Day: the single lonely people who drank their loneliness away or the couples that came in unable to get into a decent restaurant. The couples that ate tipped enough for Farah to be able to pay the next month's rent and bills.

All night she kept an eye on Penny and Brooke. Guys from Las Vegas U had a reputation of drugging girls. Farah tried to watch Mike, but it was useless. Between the drink orders and her not knowing who was who on the team, she couldn't keep her any safer.

Farah sat in the back seat of Lucas's car, leaning forward, listening to his and Thomas's conversation. Ever since university started, Lucas turned into an absent friend. He was always there when Farah or Penny needed him. He only worked twice a week for a few hours; basketball took up all the free time he had. He worked harder than anyone else on the team; he fought harder than anyone else to stay on the team.

Lucas exhaled a breath of air, nervous. "Has Penny said anything about her date tonight?"

Farah stared at Lucas, watching him rub his pant leg with an open palm. He was panicking.

Farah's eyes shot open as he shot her head back. "No way. You like Penny. How did I not know this? She wasn't with the Mike I'm thinking of, right?"

Both of the guys looked at each other, and Farah's stomach started to turn.

"Why did you guys let her go with him?" Farah raised her hand to swat Lucas on the back of the head.

Thomas grabbed Farah's arm. "We never took our eyes off of him."

"Are they safe with Rob?" Farah scolded out of frustration. She yanked her arm back to her body, hugging her middle.

Lucas blurted out his answer. "Yes. Rob would knock him out if he sees Mike put anything in either of their drinks. Penny is basically his buffer. Brooke wouldn't go if Penny didn't go."

Farah leaned back in the seat. "Then, no, Penny had a horrible time. She knows the same stories I do."

"Good." Lucas had a small smile on his face.

Farah crossed her arms, leaning back in the seat she let out a puff of air. Lucas sped the car up to get to the condo faster. Maybe it was to see her, but it might also be to make sure both of them got home okay. Farah's blood was boiling. The guys were able to watch them at the bar, but what if something happened on the way there or on the way back.

Penny's smart, she would know not to leave her drink at the table with certain guys around. Luckily and surprisingly, the girls were open about what guys to watch out for.

Anyone who needs to drug someone to get laid needed to get hit by a car. Farah puffed out air, blowing her bangs away, lost in her thoughts.

Lucas parked his car on the side of the road. All of them jumped out making a beeline to the front entrance. Lucas pulled the door open, then she ran to the opened elevator door, waiting for Thomas and Lucas to get in.

Watching the numbers light up, waiting for the sixth floor felt like an eternity. Finally, the numbers lit up, and Farah charged out of the elevator, jogging to down the hallway to the last door.

Farah opened the door, and bouquets of roses and lilies were scattered around the living room.

Penny was standing in the room with a smile. Farah ran up to her, wrapping her arms around her shoulder, holding her. "If I would have known it was that Mike, I never would have let you go."

Penny sighed, pulling away. "I let you believe it was the good Mike. Brooke needed a night."

"What the hell is this?" Lucas looked dumbfounded.

"There's a card."

Thomas walked up to Penny and ripped it out of her hand. "Farah, love, your secret admirer."

Brooke walked out of her bedroom with Rob following behind, pulling his shirt over his head. "I bet you anything, it was Brett. What did he say? I'm not finished yet?"

Rob walked up to Lucas, giving him a pound hug, and they whispered something in each other's ears.

The room looked ridiculous, but in such an amazing way. Whoever did this took months in planning and saving.

"Brett doesn't know where I live." Farah picked up a rose, smelling it.

"But! He's friends with those two." Brooke pointed at the guys.

Thomas pushed out a laugh, then walked over to Rob, whispering back and forth.

"I can't believe someone did this for me," Farah whispered loud enough for everyone to hear. She picked up a bouquet and walked back to her room.

Chapter 3

This morning Farah woke up staring at the flowers that were delivered the night before. Whoever did this either asked around or knows her well. The only guys that knew her favourite flower was Lucas and Thomas. From what she knows, Lucas likes Penny and Thomas would never do anything like that for a girl. That leaves her with the fact that someone asked them.

They know who did this; she needed to find out.

Walking down the hall to her next class, the rumors were flooding. Someone leaked that she got flowers. Names were being thrown around, and half of them she didn't even recognize.

Brett stepped out in front of Farah. "Did you get my present? It was left at your apartment."

Farah's mouth dropped. Brooke was right. Farah gave Brett a huge hug. "I loved it! About that date?"

Brett stepped back from the hug to look at her. "I can pick you up tonight at seven?"

Farah nodded her head with a smile.

She stepped into class, taking her usual spot in the back. The whispering never stopped, but this time it was from the basketball players. Thankfully, Professor Anderson started the lecturer, distracting everyone.

Thomas swooped in the seat next to Farah. He slouched in his seat, chewing on his pen. "I heard from the grapevine you have a date."

Farah rolled her eyes, typing every word Professor Anderson said. "I said yes half an hour ago, how did the leeches hear about it so fast?"

"He was bragging about being the first guy on campus getting to sleep with you."

Farah pulled her hands from the keyboard and glared at Thomas. "Seriously?"

"That's not what he said exactly."

"You're a dick."

"You love me anyways."

Farah focused back on the lecture; she tried to focus. Farah and Thomas never knew each other well, but all their history didn't matter when they were together. Everything was easy.

She looked up from the corner of her eye, watching him. In a split second, he went from being her best friend to her having the urge to lean over the seat and kiss him. In a year and a half, she never noticed how captivating he actually was. Thoughts flashed through her mind that is anything but familiar between them. Farah turned her head to look at him. She had a yearning expression. He turned toward her, pulling the pen out of his mouth. He met her eyes with a smile on his face. Farah parted her lips; butterflies formed in her stomach.

Farah shut her laptop and stood up to get out of class as fast as she could.

What the hell was that?

*****

The rest of the day she avoided her friends and any hallways Thomas would be going down. If they had the same class together, she went ten minutes late, hoping he was on time for once. She sat in different seats, doing everything she could to avoid him. She skipped lunch and studied in the library, knowing he wouldn't step foot in there. Avoiding your best friend isn't easy, but she managed not to see him. What she felt earlier in the day was everything she was against.

"Why are you avoiding us?" Brooke opened Farah's bedroom door with Penny following close behind.

"I'm not avoiding anyone." Farah turned around, fixing her makeup, waiting for Brett to show up.

"You look hot. You're also a horrible liar," Penny said with her eyes squinted.

Farah took a deep breath; Penny can call out anyone's bullshit.

The doorbell rang, and Farah flew up from her vanity chair. She was saved. She eagerly got to the door, undecided if she is excited or not.

Farah opened the door to Brett standing wide-eyed. "Whoa, flowers."

"I can't wrap my head around how you knew I loved lilies."

"I asked around. Let's go."

Farah spun around, looking at Penny. Penny stood staring at the back of Brett's head. Farah mouthed *"Knock it off,"* before shutting the door.

The ride to the restaurant was tense. She didn't want to be there, and Brett could sense it.

"Where are you taking me?"

"Burger World." He signaled and turned into the parking lot.

For someone who was able to find out her favorite flower, somehow he missed the message that Farah was a lacto-ovo-vegetarian. Farah smiled and unclipped her seat belt. Farah opened the driver's door, a bit disappointed that he never opened the car door for her.

Do guys even do that anymore? Did they ever really do that? Farah thought.

Brett opened the door for her. She walked in, giving him a friendly smile. At least one door was opened for her. All the tables were vacant. No one was seated except two families. Brett followed the server, and Farah followed Brett.

The server left two menus, but Brett spoke before she could leave. "We will just get two deluxe burgers."

Farah's mouth dropped open.

"What do you want to drink?"

"Actually, I'm a vegetarian, and since you just ordered for me, I'm going to go." Farah scooted out of the booth, not looking at Brett or the shocked look from the server.

Farah got on the closest city bus and rode to Off the Strip, hoping one of her friends were working so they can supply her with alcohol. She sat in the back of the bus mortified about how bad her date went and they weren't even a half hour in. Maybe him taking her to a burger place was her fault; you can't look at someone and know they don't eat meat.

She rang the bell to get off the bus stop right in front of her work. Her stilettos hit the sidewalk, and the breeze blew through her hair. With only one thing in mind, she charged inside.

The door opened, and the familiar smell of grease hung in the air, which came from the deep-fried food ordered from the meat-eating vultures.

"Oh no," Lucas said a little bit too loud. He started mixing a Blushing Lady, reading Farah's mind.

"Keep them coming." She sat down on the barstool that her friends normally accompany when they were off shift.

Lucas sat the martini glass in front of her.

Farah picked it up taking a large gulp.

"Spill it."

"He took me to Burger World, then ordered for me. I left."

"Did it ever occur to you he wasn't the secret admirer?"

"No, I never eat at lunch. No one would have suspected it."

Thomas walked around the bar, dropping the rag beside Farah, cleaning up the rings from the glasses. "You gave it up pretty easy and fast."

Farah shot Thomas a glare.

"My brother called. The furnace in the building is out. Mind if we crash with you three tonight?"

Farah stared at Thomas with a blank face. That is the last thing she needed after her thoughts earlier in the day. "You have a brother?"

"Three. So, can we or not?"

Farah, still staring at him, was trying to fight against her urges. Maybe her date failed because she wanted it to. The more she looked at him, the more she needed him.

"Yeah, it's fine. Wouldn't be the first sleepover. Just stay out of Brooke's room this time."

Lucas replaced Farah's drink. She never even realized he made her another one. "And Penny's."

Thomas smiled smugly. "That just leaves you, Farah."

"I'll sleep on the couch."

"Oh, come on. I wouldn't try to sleep with you anyways."

Farah put her head down. That really shouldn't have stung her as much as it did. "Lucas can you ring me in spinach dip, please?"

Three drinks later Farah stumbled into the apartment laughing, with Lucas and Thomas following behind her with clothes for the next two days. Alcohol had always hit her harder and faster than everyone else. Drinking on an empty stomach made it worse. Brooke and Penny were sitting at the kitchen island studying. They both looked up annoyed, then their faces turned into amusement, holding back laughter.

"What the hell happened to you?" Penny couldn't hold back the laughter.

"Bad date." Farah laughed.

Lucas walked up to Penny filling her in. Instantly, Penny wrapped her arms around him. Farah looked up at Brooke, who shrugged her shoulders.

Thomas leaned into Farah, whispering in her ear. He put his hand on the arch of her back. The smell of his cologne intoxicated her. "I need a pillow and blanket."

Farah let out a low humming noise, him being so close to her was exactly what she wanted. He was just saying the wrong words.

"Take my bed. I'll stay on the couch. I need to change. Stay out here."

Farah walked to her bedroom, holding out her hand, using the wall to help steady her. Every attempt in avoiding him, all the success she had blew up in her face. The first door on the left was her bedroom. The door was still opened wide, showing everyone who walked toward the bathroom the clothes on the floor. She shut the door and walked to her vanity, pulling out a makeup wipe. She wiped away every attempt that she put into herself to look good for a date that she never wanted. Feeling obligated to do something was her normal. She thought she let go of that when she ripped up the application. It isn't that easy to let go of something. She kicked off her stilettos, stripped off her jeans, and pulled her shirt over her head. She bent over, picking up a pair of spandex shorts and a tank top. Thankfully, she never over drank. Common sense hasn't left her.

She grabbed a pillow from the bed and a blanket from the closet. She opened the bedroom door and the sounds of her friends laughing filled the air.

"I'm done."

Farah got in the view of the kitchen to see Penny tugging on Lucas hand toward her bedroom. Brooke stood up to go to her room.

Thomas walked up to Farah. Without thinking, Farah put her hand on his chest. He caught his breath. Farah's heart beat rapidly. He stepped closer to her, making her body tremble. She swallowed hard. "Good night." She was about to pull her hand away when he grabbed it, holding her hand between his two hands.

"Stay in your bed. I won't try anything." He held on to her hand tighter.

Farah pulled it away with every bit of strength she had in her body. Whatever these feelings were, they needed to go away. "You've told me once or twice."

"Now you just have to trust me." Thomas grabbed Farah's hand.

She wanted to be stubborn, but his skin on hers felt too good to turn away from. Thomas reached his arm around the corner of the hallway into the kitchen, flicking the light off. Farah fought against his grasp to get away. He loosened his grip for her. She dropped the extra blanket while tossing the pillow on the bed. Farah watched Thomas undress from the reflection in the vanity mirror. He took off his shirt, revealing the muscles on his back. He stripped off his jeans; his muscle flexed as he moved, only making it harder for Farah to look away. He put on his black-and-white plaid pajama bottoms, then turned around, looking at Farah staring at him in the mirror.

Farah moved her face to the side, feeling embarrassed, ashamed and pathetic for ever seeing him more than a friend. He's probably used this line multiple times. Lucas wouldn't stop him if it meant a night with Penny.

Farah turned around, moving her books off the bed, stacking them into a pile. She stood up and flicked the light switch, making it dark. She crawled into bed beside him. She was trying to keep her distance, almost falling off the bed.

Any alcohol that was in her system seemed to be soaked up from the humiliation of being on the worst date she's ever been on, just to be fully clothed and sharing a bed with the alluring Thomas Johansson. She didn't know what one was worse.

"You can come closer to me," Thomas muffled into his pillow.

Farah shook her head, forgetting that he couldn't see her. Somewhere between spending every day with each other, working with each other, and taking the same classes, Farah fell hard for Thomas. Bottling up her feelings for so long, they were bound to hit her. Guilt was the next emotion to come. She was so cold for Brooke for having a crush on him.

"Farah." Thomas put his hand on her back.

Farah's entire body became weak. She shot out of bed, grabbing the pillow. Guys at school seem to be dying for a date with her, but the one person she wanted friend zoned her a long time ago. "I'm going to sleep on the couch."

The bed creaked. Suddenly, Farah was blinded by the bedroom light.

"Jesus, that's bright." Thomas blinked hard. "Just stay, please."

"I've had a really bad night, and I don't need you to tell me for the third time how unattractive I am." Farah laughed once. "I'm surprised you are even willing to share a bed with me."

"I don't sleep with—" Thomas bit his tongue. "Just come to bed. We have to wake up in a few hours. We don't have time for this."

Thomas grabbed Farah's arm, dragging her toward her bed. He stood in front of her, pushing on her shoulders to make her sit down. Farah's arm tingled from his touch. He let go, but she could still feel his hands on her.

She lay down, rolling over to face him. "Is your furnace really out, or was this just an elaborate plan to make me feel like shit?"

"It's fucking freezing in there. If you would have come up with us, you would have known for yourself. If anyone feels like shit, it's me."

"Why?"

"Good night, Farah."

Thomas put his hand behind Farah's head, pulling her forehead down for him to kiss it. Farah gasped at his touch, his soft lips hovering over her skin. His breathing deepened. He pulled his mouth away. His hand was still tangled up in her hair. Farah was frozen.

Thomas lowered his hand down her back, pulling her closer to his chest. Farah nuzzled her face into his skin, his fingers running down her back. Nothing would be able to compare to the feeling that she had in that moment.

Farah pushed away from him. She felt Thomas's head moved down to look at her. She scooted her body up, leaning her forehead against his. She leaned in, touching his lips to hers. No hesitation, she opened her mouth with her body becoming weaker and weaker.

Farah felt Thomas pull away. She put her hand to her lips, trying to remember what he tasted like. "I'm so sorry."

"You're drunk, just go to bed." Thomas growled, rolling over.

Lying on her back with her hand on her mouth, a tear rolled down her temples, hitting her pillow. These feelings came out of nowhere, hitting her all at once, only for her to get rejected. She grabbed her pillow, picking the blanket off the floor, and walked to the couch.

Lying down, she felt miles away from the one place she wanted to be.

Chapter 4

"Oh, you look like shit." Penny sat down, putting Farah's legs over her lap. "Did you sleep at all?"

Farah sniffled her nose. "I'm probably going to skip today."

"You never slept then?"

Farah shook her head, fighting back the tears that wanted to escape. Penny stood up, putting Farah's feet on the floor, holding out her hand. Farah grabbed her hand. The nice thing about their friendship was that neither of them pried. They would talk when they were ready to talk. Unlike Brooke. She knew boundaries. Brooke would nag until she got an answer that she was satisfied with.

Brooke opened her bedroom door fully dressed. Her makeup was done better than any other day. Her dark-brown hair was straightened.

"What's wrong with you?"

Farah walked over to the fridge, pulling out a container of raspberries. "Couch sucks to sleep on."

"You could have come in my bed."

Farah turned around and saw Thomas staring at her. She set the raspberries down on the counter and walked over to him, nodding to her bedroom. With hesitation, he followed her in.

Farah leaned against the door, shutting it, trying to find the words through her exhaustion. "I was out of line last night."

"Just don't drink anymore while I'm here. I don't want you to be doing things you don't mean."

Farah nodded while she tried to figure out what the hell was that supposed to mean. "Did you sleep?"

"No."

Farah picked up his bag up off the ground. "I'll go to class. You have a game tonight. Stay here and try to rest."

Farah tossed the bag on the bed, turning around so Thomas could change. Ignoring her mind, telling her to turn around and watch him strip down to his boxers. She heard the bag hit the ground and felt his hand on her arm, pulling her down to the mattress. Farah squealed, then busted out in laughter when she bounced off the sheets. Thomas covered her with the blanket and pulled her in close.

"I will never try to kiss you again." Farah had to push out the words, mostly convincing herself.

"Don't be so sure of yourself." Thomas laughed.

Farah's eyes got heavy, her breathing evened out, and she fell asleep.

*****

Thomas moved his arm from Farah's shoulder. She opened one eye, watching him roll over. He hit his phone with his hand a few times, trying to swipe the alarm away. Thomas pulled his other arm out from under her, and disappointment hit her. It felt way too good to be that close to him.

"What time is it?" Farah kicked her legs off the bed, leaning into her knees.

"Almost noon. Get ready, we can go get a coffee and make it to history." Thomas deep voice sent goose bumps down Farah's arms, making the hair stand up.

Farah nodded, trying to not look disappointed. She knew she needed to go to class, but that never stopped her from wishing they never had to leave the four walls of her bedroom. Farah stood up, sitting at her vanity, rushing through her makeup.

"I look like shit," Farah muttered.

Thomas laughed, putting on his jeans, then fell on the bed. "Shut up."

"Rude."

"How's your hang over?"

"Nonexistent." Farah sprayed her face with setting spray. "Shame is a really good way to sober up. Did you know that?"

Thomas stood up from the bed, pulling a shirt over his head. He turned around, staring at the orange lily, rose bouquet sitting on the dresser. "If you are going to kiss me, kiss me when you're sober."

"And go through that again? No, thank you."

"I'll be the drunk one tonight, so don't be taking advantage of me."

"Ten bucks says you won't even come back here."

"Fifty says I will." He opened the bedroom door, turning around. "You better have the cash. I haven't slept with anyone in months."

*****

Thomas and Farah got out of his car walking up the pathway to the cafeteria. Like usual their friends were seated at the same table, but extra attention was drawn to them as they walked in. The news of her date last night spread around, plus walking in alone with Thomas late gave people more ideas.

Thomas set the drink tray down in front of Lucas. Lucas read the cups, giving them to the right person. Lucas looked at Thomas. Farah quickly moved her eyes to Thomas fast enough to see him shake his head.

"You guys were pretty cuddled up when we left this morning." Penny smirked. "What was that about?"

Farah sat down, taking a sip of her soy cappuccino. "Absolutely nothing." The words left Farah's mouth, and she instantly regretted lying to the human lie detector.

Penny glanced over to Thomas, who was picking the sleeve of his cup. Her lips turned upwards. "Mhmm."

"Why did you get a D?"

Farah shot a glare to Brooke.

"You left a paper on the couch."

Farah still wasn't sure how she felt about Brooke, but her bitchy personality was too much to handle. She was Penny's friend first and somehow made her way into the group.

"What classes?" Thomas leaned in, giving Farah all of his attention.

"History and math." Farah knew the truth was going to come out but not when she was so mentally exhausted.

"Get your shifts covered this weekend. How the hell did I not know? I sit next to you every single day."

"It's not your job to babysit her," Brooke mumbled.

"Just shut up, Brooke," Lucas scolded.

"Why did you get a D?" This was one reason why Farah couldn't stand Brooke; she never knew when to shut up.

Thomas looked at Farah. Farah gave him a nod.

"She decided it was time to go against her parents plans."

Lucas and Penny shot a look of worry in Farah's direction. Without saying a word, they felt the same anxiety as she did.

Farah's alarm went off on her phone, telling her it was time to walk to class. Before she was able to sit up, Lucas leaned up against her.

"I need my good luck charms. Please tell me you guys will be there tonight."

Penny reached out for his hand. "You know we work tonight. Someone has to make the victory drinks, after you kick state's ass."

*****

"Are you ever going to tell me what the hell is happening with Thomas?" Penny asked.

Farah stopped to look around, and the only person who was in earshot was their boss Kale. The rest of tables at the bar were empty. Everyone was at the game. As soon as they win or lose, people were going to trickle in, then the teammates are going to come in at once, overwhelming the bartenders.

Farah sighed, annoyed with Penny's loud whispers. "Nothing is happening. What you saw were two friends sleeping in the same bed."

"Bullshit. He was talking to you, and it was like you were absorbed by him."

"Absorbed by who?" Kale rushed over to listen to Penny's gossip. Being their manager for so long, he was more like a friend to all five of them. He had light buzzed-cut hair and dark-green eyes. He was average looking, but his tattoo sleeve gave him a few extra bonus points.

"Thomas," Penny said wide-eyed, staring at Farah.

Kale looked like his eyes were going to pop out of his head. "No way."

"She still hasn't denied it yet."

Farah was saved to the door opening and a crowd of people walking in with orange-and-red face paint. From their loud behavior, it was a dead giveaway that they won. Farah bet $200 on this game. Living in Vegas, all of the kids from other cities wanted the full gambling experience and bets were always placed. It made the game more interesting to those who didn't know what was happening, and it was easy cash to some people who paid attention to the game. Farah, Brooke, and Penny have lost a lot of money betting on Vegas U. They still took the chance on not beating against their best friends.

Brooke came in under Rob's arm. He kissed her, then patted her ass before she came rushing to the back of the bar. "Lucas got the winning basket. Farah, I'm taking your shifts this weekend. Thomas was nagging me."

Penny's face light up as she opened a beer bottle.

"Uh, hey, Farah."

Farah looked up to see Brett standing in front of him with his hands in his pockets. "I feel bad about last night. I was just nervous. Is there any way you can give me another chance?"

Farah opened his Corona, then dropped a lime in it deep in thought. He was a better option than Thomas. "Ask me Monday."

Brett offered her a small smile before walking away.

"Why would you tell him that?" Penny stood close to Farah, whispering in her ear.

"Because I actually have a chance with him."

Penny backed up with big eyes. "I knew it."

A half hour of mixing drinks, opening beer bottles, and being completely distracted, everyone in the bar had a drink in their hands. The tip jars were full. People were oddly generous when they won their bets.

Thomas slammed down a wad of cash on the bar. "Breakfast is on you then?"

"Or you, our bet is still on."

"May as well give me the money now."

Thomas wasn't even trying to charm her, but Farah found herself consumed by him. She reached on the bar to grab her money. Her hand slid next to his, and her entire body became weak. Farah shoved the bills in her apron, swallowing hard. *I'm in trouble,* she thought.

Like any other game night, the hours passed by fast. The number of sober people in the bar started dropping, people got kicked out, cabs got called. When the team wins, there was never a fight. When the team loses, fights break out. Mostly from the players that got in on sport scholarships. Kale locked the front doors, leaving a few other bartenders that Farah never knew very well, herself, Penny, Brooke, Thomas, and Lucas.

"Is the room spinning for anyone else?" Lucas set his hands on his head.

"Just you, bud." Kale put his hand on his back. He stared at Thomas long enough for him to turn around and look at him. When Kale got Thomas's attention, Kale gave him a nod.

What's with these people's gestures today?

Farah grabbed the counting sheet. She went to the back, slipped on a jacket, then walked into the back cooler. Counting beer is the most tedious thing she has ever forced herself to do. She usually has to recount twice because her basic math skills aren't there. After a half hour, she walked to the front rubbing her hands together.

"Come on, Rob's waiting for me." Brooke slipped on her jacket, walking to the door.

They all piled in Farah's car, crossing their fingers that the engine will start. When it started, Brooke let out a puff of air. The ride home was filled with Lucas groaning. Whatever way the car turned, his body swayed that way. In four years of friendship, she has only seen Lucas drunk a handful of times. He was never sick drunk like he was that night.

Thomas reached in Farah's purse at his feet, opening her wallet. "I'll take my fifty now."

Farah laughed. "You never even talked to a girl tonight, and you're sober. Are you broken?"

"You could say that."

"Brett asked her out again."

Farah looked at Penny in the review mirror, glaring at her.

Penny's eyes were locked on Thomas, watching him. "She told him to ask her on Monday."

31

Farah pulled up in her parking spot before Penny could say anything else, making the car ride even more uncomfortable.

The elevator opened. Brooke charged to the apartment door, hugging Rob. They both acted like it was months since they have seen each other. She used her key to open the door. All of them piled in, and Farah was happy that their place was big enough to handle so many people.

Farah walked to the fridge, grabbing tzatziki. She opened the cupboard to grab pita bread, then dropped it on the island for Lucas. "Eat this."

Lucas nodded and started to mow down on the food.

Thomas put his hand on the arch of Farah's back. She sunk into him.

"What are you going to say to Brett?" Penny leaned into the bar, staring at Farah and Thomas.

"I was kind of a bitch. Maybe I should? I don't know. I'm going to bed." Farah walked past Thomas. He never took her hand off her back until he couldn't reach her any longer.

She walked back to the room, still feeling his touch on her. She looked at the bed. The covers were just how the both of them left them. She knew that even if they did end up together, they wouldn't last. His friendship meant more to her. Her feelings would pass, and that would be the end of it. She grabbed her pajamas and walked to the bathroom for a shower.

She got back in her room with Thomas shirtless in his pajama pants staring at the roof. She crawled in bed with her back facing him. She pulled up the covers and felt his body heat radiating off him. He rolled onto his side, wrapping his arm around her, pulling her closer to his body.

She could feel his breathing on her neck, making her tingle in places she forgot existed. He held her closer, bringing his lips to her neck. Farah inhaled deeply. The tingling only became more intense. She felt his pants rise. Thomas moved his hand down to Farah's hip, gently thrusting against her.

She wanted to roll over and face him, but Thomas rolled on his back, grunted, then stood up and shut the door behind him.

The pipes from the shower complained from water running through them. Farah rolled on her back, looking into the dark room. Her thoughts consumed her. Everything about Thomas was too welcoming for her. He was too familiar. Him sleeping in her bed was an awful idea, but waking up to him was better than anything she ever felt.

The door opened a crack, and Thomas ran in, shutting the door behind him, shivering. "Jesus, fuck." He yanked the blanket from her, crawling in the bed. He lay on his back.

Farah was still staring at the roof. "If you were drunk, I would tell you that the shame would sober you up."

"Shame? You're hands down the most beautiful women I've ever seen."

A smile spread across Farah's face. Butterflies turned into something else, something more real. As terrified as she was, everything felt so perfect. "You're not so bad yourself."

Chapter 5

Farah woke up to an empty bed. She sat up, put on her fuzzy bunny slippers, and dragged her feet to the kitchen. As soon as the door opened, she heard four voices chatting. Brooke saw her coming. She poured Farah a cup of coffee and set her vanilla almond milk creamer next to her cup with a spoon.

Farah was taken aback by Brooke's actions, so she just gave her a tired smile. "Where's Thomas?"

Lucas looked at Penny, then at Farah, trying not to smile. "He'll be back."

"How's your hangover?"

"Killer."

Farah sat in the chair, stirring her coffee, dreading the weekend of tutoring.

Halfway through her cup, the door of the apartment opened.

"I come bearing breakfast."

Thomas's voice made a smile on Farah's face instantly. She raised her cup to her mouth, trying to hide her lips curving upward.

He took a step behind Farah and put his hand on her back. "Wrap with salsa, egg, and red pepper."

Farah turned around to look up at him. For a split second, they locked eyes and she felt more peace than she ever felt. Without a word said, she put her arm around his waist, giving him a one-armed hug. He pulled her in closer, taking a deep breath.

Farah let go as soon as Rob started talking.

"If I didn't know better—" He was cut off when someone threw a hash brown at him.

Farah cleared her throat. "Let's start studying now."

Farah led Thomas into her room. "You're probably going to be going home tonight. What is it, forty-eight hours until they have to fix the furnace?"

Thomas laughed once. "You looked it up, didn't you? If you wanted me gone, you could have just said so."

"I just don't know how long this is going to take." Farah shrugged her shoulders. "Might be easier if you just stay over again." The words left her mouth, and she hoped that it wasn't too eager.

She looked up at Thomas; he was trying to fight a smile.

*****

After hours of Thomas dumbing down both math and history, Farah was finally able to grasp them for the first time all semester. He helped her with two papers that were due Monday. If a pop quiz was to happen, she would have been ready enough to confidently pass with a grade higher.

Hearing how smart Thomas was made him so much sexier to Farah. She already knew he was smart, but witnessing it firsthand just made him so much more appealing.

"I need water and food. Want anything?" Thomas stood from her bed.

"Just water."

Her phone vibrated on the bed beside her. Farah moved her arm to pick it up. She flipped it over, seeing a video call from Braelynn. She answered, holding the phone up.

Braelynn squealed. "Oh my god, I miss you." She was wearing her camo jacket with their last name "Whitmore" embossed onto it.

"Brae! Is Kai with you?"

Braelynn shook her head no. Farah wiped a tear that ran down her cheek. She would do just about anything to see them both. They all look identical. Braelynn shares the same long hair. When she is on tour, it's pulled back in a bun. Kai's black hair is shaved.

"When are you guys coming home?" asked Farah.

"Two weeks!"

Seeing her made every emotion hit Farah. The life they have was set up to be her life. Even though she was positive her petite frame would never pass the physical. It never helped fill her with the fear of making the wrong choices.

"Farah, what's wrong?"

"I'm telling Mom and Dad I'm not joining."

"Me and Kai figured so. I'm insanely proud of you."

"Farah! I'm ordering pizza!" Thomas shouted.

Braelynn's eyebrows shot up. "Who was that?"

"Thomas."

"Have you admitted that you like him yet?"

Farah pulled her knees up to her chest, not looking at the screen.

"Ha! It's only been a year. It's a long-time coming, baby sister."

"Shut up, I miss you."

"Be home soon, I love you. I'll call you when I land."

Braelynn hung up. Just like that, Farah was left with the fear of not seeing them again.

Thomas landed on the bed with his phone. "Who was that?"

"My sister. How much did you hear?"

"Just that she loved you."

Farah let out a breath of air from her lungs. She didn't understand how her sister knew she had feelings for Thomas before Farah even knew she had feelings for Thomas. He was a disaster waiting to happen.

"Let's go watch a movie." Farah pushed herself off the mattress, walking to the door.

Thomas put her hand on Farah's shoulder and spun her around, giving her a gentle push to the wall. Farah stood looking at Thomas. She watched the dedication in his eyes. Every thought she had about him consuming her was wrong. She had no idea what it felt like to be completely consumed by him. Her heart began to race, beating against her ribcage. Having him so close to her with this look in his eyes was all she needed to know that this was more than a crush. He put his hand under her chin. He raised it up and kissed her. Thomas was just as eager to feel her tongue inside his mouth as Farah was. He moved his hand to the back of her hair, tangling his fingers. She wrapped her arms around his waist, pulling him in as close as possible.

Thomas hummed. He pulled away slowly. "It took me eight months to save for your flowers." He gave her a quick peck. "Then you went on a date with another guy."

Farah stood, looking at Thomas in amazement. Her body became completely still. He was the last person on earth she ever suspected to do anything like that for a girl. Seeing this entire new side of him, she felt herself falling harder for him. Any chance of her fighting or denying her feelings was long gone.

"Did your furnace actually stop working?"

Thomas looked around and shook his head. "I was losing you before I even had you."

Farah busted out in laughter, wrapping her arms around his middle, pulling him in close. "Well played."

The front door of the apartment opened, and Farah wasn't sure if she should drop her arms or not. "I guess back to reality."

Thomas put his hand in Farah's hair, pulling her head to his chest. "They are going to look at me and know something happened. Are you sure you want to be that girl?"

"Am I that girl?"

"Not since the second I laid eyes on you."

*****

Monday morning, Farah was more aware of the eyes on Thomas than ever. Even though she knew every girl wasn't staring at him, she felt like they were. They decided Saturday night to take things slow and just see where it took them. Thomas left that night, leaving her bed empty and alone.

Farah groaned, looking down at the table, as a busty blonde walked up to Thomas.

"I hear you're still taking your leap of abstinence. What's that about?"

Farah knowing that this girl came in and out of his room dozens of times only made her more uncomfortable.

"Hey." Brett came up behind her. Farah whipped around in her chair, already done with the day. "You said to ask you Monday."

Farah felt a set of eyes on her from the back of her head. She knew Thomas was sitting there, staring at her, waiting for the moment of truth. "No." She shifted in her seat. "I think I'm kind of with someone."

Brett spun around, shaking his head. Farah can still hear Thomas turning down the girl behind her.

Farah pushed up from the chair, walking around the table. She put her hand on the side of the girl, shoving her to the side. Farah straddled Thomas's lap. Not waiting for him to protest, she put her lips on his. Farah put her arms around his shoulders, and he placed his hands on her hips. She meant it to be a quick kiss, both of them are telling the entire cafeteria that they belong to each other, but each second that passed by she found herself being molded into him more and more. His zipper was barely able to contain him.

Thomas pulled away to catch his breath. "You're killing me. Jesus, only my girlfriend could kiss me like that in front of everyone and not be embarrassed."

Farah casually walked back to the other side of the table, reaching for his hand. "Girlfriend? So much for taking to slow."

Brett scoffed. "I lost a girl to Johansson."

Thomas squeezed Farah's hand tighter, a flick of rage flashed in his eyes. "Back the fuck up."

"You're no different from the rest, Farah. When he gets bored of you, call me."

Farah flew out of her seat right as Thomas stood up. She rushed over to the side of the table, meeting him halfway. She linked fingers with his. As soon as he registered he was holding her hand, he looked down. Farah went on her tippy toes and kissed him. She pulled away, walking back to the other side of the table glaring at Brett.

Penny, Brooke, and Lucas sat there looking shocked at their friend's sudden burst of rage. Not once in the time they have known Thomas to be that pissed off.

Penny watched him walk off. "Turd nugget."

Her friends all started laughing; a few of the other basketballs players in earshot smirked.

Thomas stretched out his fingers. "I'm shaking. I have to go to class before I knock him out. Coming, babe?"

Thomas just tossed that nickname out like it was the most natural thing in the world. Farah was so hell bent on thinking that having a crush on him would be the end of the world, little did she know, that was her way of repressing her feelings.

Farah stood up after Thomas. He walked around the table, wrapping his arm around her shoulder, hugging her. Farah reached on her shoulder interlocking their fingers.

The entire walk to class neither of them spoke. Farah was too wrapped up in her mind. What if Brett was right? He was going to get tired of her, then she'll be thrown to the side like every other girl. If one thing was certain, Thomas never dated. She tried to think back to the conversations they had. He never once mentioned an ex-girlfriend.

Thomas opened the door for Farah, and she took the regular seats in the back. Thomas turned his body, looking at her. Farah wasn't able to meet his eyes.

"You know that's bullshit, right?"

Farah looked around the room, noting how empty the auditorium was. "Is it? If this thing blows up, we lost our friendship and divide everyone."

"I've wanted you for too long. I don't care what it takes to keep you."

"You say that now."

"I mean it."

Farah leaned over giving Thomas a peck. Voices filled the room around them. She slouched in her chair, holding his hand. Every few moments Thomas would squeeze her hand.

She let out a sigh, already feeling the heartbreak creeping up.

Chapter 6

Penny ripped the earbuds out of Farah's ears. The sound of forgotten music from the early 2000s blasted out of them. Penny fell on her back onto Farah's bed, swinging her legs up in the air.

"I need to ask this. Don't hate me."

Farah blew a loose strand of her hair, interlocking her ankles with Penny.

"What's it like dating someone who slept with your friends?"

The words left Penny's mouth, forcing Farah to think about something she was dreading. She dropped her legs. Her calves hit the mattress hard. She reached up behind her, grabbing the pillow, pressing it on her face.

Farah lifted the corner of the pillow to let her voice be heard. "I hate it. I hate it. I hate it."

"You've fallen for him, haven't you?" Penny waited for Farah's response.

Farah couldn't say how she felt because it felt too soon. It felt crazy.

"I knew it. You fell in love."

Farah ripped the pillow off her face, raising her eyebrows at her.

She was getting sick and tired of everyone knowing how she felt, before she was able to admit it to herself.

"I'm an idiot. I'm setting myself up to be hurt."

Penny picked up the earbuds, passing one to Farah. The playlist played twice. Both of them lay on the bed in silence, just like high school.

The door of the apartment opened. Footsteps walked down the hall. The next thing Farah knew her lips were against Thomas's. She saw him at school four hours ago, but she missed his lips more than ever. Dating your best friend was scary enough, but falling in love with him was terrifying.

She pulled away, gazing into his brown iris. The first time she saw him flashed before her eyes. He was wearing a royal-blue sweater. It was half zipped up, revealing his black wife beater, with a tattoo on his chest. Every time he shifted his body, more of it would show, just not enough for her to see what it was. She remembered her heart fluttering. The feelings hit her before she even knew his name.

Farah blinked hard before looking away. The reality set in that her friends know too much of his body. Farah instantly felt sick to her stomach.

The bed squeaked as Penny stood up, leaving them alone.

Thomas tucked Farah's hair behind her ear. "What's wrong?"

"How are you able to date me knowing you slept with our friends? How is Lucas and Rob okay with you being around them so much?" Farah's heart rate sped up. She was regretting the words before she even said them. "I can't be with someone who's screwed around with them." Farah's eyes began to flood with tears.

"Fuck." Thomas stood up, not taking his eyes from Farah. He put his hands on his head, interlocking his fingers.

Tears fell from Farah's eyes. She wiped them away, feeling ridiculous crying over someone when it hasn't even been a week.

He sat on the bed in front of her. He put his hands on her cheeks, wiping away a tear. "Don't do this."

"What do you expect me to do? You claim you saved eight months to surprise me when I know for a fact you didn't spend every night alone? I'm such an idiot for feeling this way about you."

Thomas stood up, standing on the other side of the bedroom. Farah flinched, seeing the anger flash in his eyes. Thomas raised his voice, reflecting how he felt.

"Eight months I've been trying to convince myself that I might be good enough for you. I was alone every single night until I slept in your bed. Don't push my past in my face."

Farah stood up, frustrated, shouting back at him. "You haven't even slept with me! How are you able to say you won't get bored of me?"

"Jesus Christ, Farah! How can everyone see it but you?"

"Now I'm stupid. Awesome."

"I'm in love with you. Damn it."

Farah felt like her heart stopped. It was too early for her to say it back. She walked closer. The only thing she wanted to do was touch him.

Thomas closed his eyes, the tension from his body left. He let out a breath. The yelling was finally over. "I know this is really new. It's too early to say it. I love you. Don't walk away because I made shitty choices trying to get my mind off of the one girl I could never have."

Farah jumped on his chest, wrapping her arms around his neck. Their lips crashed together. The air changed in the room. The tension broke. Her tongue met his when he began to back up against the bed. She pulled away when he set her down.

Farah laid eyes on his belt buckle. Without missing a beat, the belt was undone and his pants were unzipped. He began to poke through his boxers. Thomas bent down, pulling Farah's tank top over her head. She stood up to kiss him. He pulled away after a peck. Thomas was as eager as Farah. In an instant, his shirt was in the corner of the room.

This time, with Thomas standing in front of her shirtless, she took the extra moment to study his body. The tattoo she remembered seeing was an elm tree over his chest that extended onto his collarbone.

He unclipped the hooks on her bra, while Farah started to undo her jeans.

Thomas leaned in to kiss her while slowly laying Farah on the bed. "I love you."

Farah's body became weak. Her knees were already shaking.

Thomas stood up and pulled his pants down to his ankles. He shut his eyes tight. "Shit, I wasn't expecting this to happen."

Farah smiled, pointing at the dresser drawer. Thomas briskly walked over to it, opening it with more force than needed. "These aren't going to work."

"I'm clean," Farah blurted out.

"Me too. Birth control?"

"For the next three years."

Thomas rushed back over, positing himself over her. He leaned down, kissing Farah's neck while listening to her hum. She raised her hands, putting them on his cheeks, pulling him in for a kiss. She bit his bottom lip.

Farah let out a gasp, realizing why the condoms weren't going to work. She noticed Thomas trying to take it slow, but the more she began to moan, the more control he lost.

Farah's legs shook as she screamed out. She raised her hips for Thomas to have better access. He slammed against her, taking a deep breath. Farah hated the thought of him already finishing.

Time was getting away from them; neither of them cared. The longer they were together, the more passionate they became.

She dropped her hips, moaning, closing her eyes. "Thomas."

He leaned down, their chest brushing against each other. Sweat was making it easier for him to slide against her. "Open your eyes."

Farah did as she was told, leaning up to kiss him. She kissed him with more passion than she ever thought she could manage. The love she felt for him in that moment was indescribable.

Thomas reached climax, pulling his lips away from her. Farah felt his body quiver against her.

He lay down beside her on the bed, trying to catch his breath. Farah looked over at the man she loved. He just didn't know it yet.

Thomas pulled her in closer, kissing her hair. "Just so you know, that was the last time you have sex for the first time."

Farah smiled. She wanted him for the rest of her life.

Chapter 7

Farah laid eyes on the old Honda Civic in the parking lot, jogging toward it with three Benjamin Franklins in her hand. She felt optimistic when she woke up, taking that as a sign to gamble big on tonight's game. She stood at the car's window, puzzled on why Civic drivers thought it was a good idea to mismatch the colors of the car's hood.

"I thought I'd see you again tonight."

Farah had no idea what his name was; all she knew was that he's a senior who used to play until he blew out his knee.

"Three hundred dollars on our boys." She flashed him the money.

"You sure you want to gamble that much on your boyfriend?"

"You just don't believe in him." Farah patted the white roof, while scrunching her nose at the black hood.

Walking back into the school, floods of students from Boulder City were being escorted to the car for their bets. If Las Vegas University pulls in another win, she just paid her rent for a few months.

Farah swung open the door at the gym entrance. She walked down the hall to see Thomas standing against the wall with two blonde girls facing him. She felt her heart drop out of her chest when one of them put her hand on his arm. She stood watching him pull her into a hug.

"Farah." Thomas jogged up to her.

For the first time since meeting him, she didn't want to be near him.

Farah couldn't shake it; it was probably nothing. She also couldn't shake the feeling of him getting bored and keeping girls on hold for backup.

That's ridiculous, she thought.

One of the girls turned around, squinting her eyes at Farah. The other one turned around with a look that could kill. That was all she needed.

Thomas reached out for her hand. Farah pulled it away before he could touch her.

"Was everything you said the other night bullshit? You say you sleeping around is in your past. It's very much in my present."

Thomas looked behind him, turning back to Farah wide-eyed. "No, you don't understand."

"No, I think I do. I'm done, Thomas." Farah turned around, fighting back the tears.

"Farah!"

The pleading in his voice broke her heart even more. This was the heart break that she was waiting for. Brooke, Penny, and Lucas all stared at her as she ran past them. Not one of her friends said a word to her.

She got out to the parking lot, unlocking the doors, running to her car. She opened the door, letting all the tears fall from her eyes. She inhaled a shaky breath, wiping her face. Putting the car in reverse, she stepped on the gas pedal, backing out.

The ride back home felt longer than it should have; the silence interrupted by her sobbing. The apartment was no different. She crawled into bed wearing the same clothes she had on before. It never took long for the pillow to be soaked from the tears. Regret hit her, which only made her cry harder.

The next morning the winning money was on the island. One thousand two hundred dollars meant that Thomas played his frustrations out or he was benched. The morning was quiet. The apartment that held five of them every day was empty. She went to work to find Brooke and Penny got their shifts covered.

The same thing happened on Sunday.

Monday came around. Once again the apartment was silent. Farah checked Brooke's room to see if she slept in. She opened the door to see the dresser drawers opened and fully empty. She went to the closet, only a few hangers left behind. Farah caught her breath. She ran the Penny's room and everything was still in its normal spots, other than her closet having less clothes in it.

By lunch, no one sent her a message. Farah stayed in the library to study. Not having Thomas around to dumb things down made everything more frustrating. She wrote on dozens of flashcards, flipping them until she got every single answer right.

Wednesday and Thursday, Farah never had the courage or confidence to get out of bed. She phoned into work, skipped classes. If she wasn't sleeping, she was staring at the roof. She was never this alone before. Growing up, she had three siblings that where always there for her. She didn't have the luxury to be able to phone Kai and Braelynn. When she did talk to them, she only gave them good news. There were circles around her eyes, and her pajamas hang off her from not having the energy to eat. She hasn't been able to answer a single one of their calls. Once a day she will hear the front door open. Penny would go to her room and leave, completely unaware that Farah was home.

On Friday she couldn't ignore her stomach growling anymore. Farah was about to open the cafeteria door for the first time all week until she heard a familiar voice shout her name. Before she had time to spin around, tears already began to fall down her face. Braelynn and Kai ran up to her. Farah wrapped her arms around her brother and sister for the first time in months. They just got off the plane still in their uniforms.

"I can't believe you're home," Farah whispered.

"Only for a few days. Come to Mom and Dad's tonight for dinner." Kai hugged her again. "You haven't told them yet, have you?"

Farah shook her head.

"Tonight then!" Braelynn smiled. "Please. We won't be able to see you much."

Farah grabbed both of their hands. "I'll be there."

*****

Farah, her siblings, and parents all sat around the table in an awkward silence. Her parents never remember that she is a vegetarian. This far into her life she thought they choose to forget. Her mother's brown hair was highlighted gray. Her father's dark-brown hair was a military approved buzz cut. Neither of her parents chose to waste a minute before asking Farah if she was dropping out of school or not.

"No," Farah said, which was muffled into her hand.

"What was that?" He father sat with perfect posture; it drove Farah insane.

"No, sir." Farah rolled her eyes. "I'm not joining."

Kai knew what was happening. Hearing his little sister talk with such an attitude caught him off guard. Braelynn and Kai are twins. If it wasn't for the year-and-a-half age difference, they would all look like triplets. Ace's photo was framed on the wall. He was the odd one out in the family with blond hair. He had Farah's emerald green eyes, making him look somewhat related to the rest of them.

"She's also dating Thomas Johansson." Braelynn tossed out the useless fact of the day.

Farah looked down at the table. "We aren't together."

Farah's mother stood up at the table, pointing at the door. "Get the hell out of our house. You're not to come back."

Farah stared at her parents in confusion. Her father got up and walked away. Both of her siblings stood up, trying to stick up for her. Farah pushed out the chair, storming to the door, tears soaking her face. After being numb for five days, she was surprised she was even able to produce any tears.

She found herself at Off the Strip. The only thing she could think about was how to make all five of their lives easier. She hoped Kale would be there, and no one else would be. With no game on, she knew it would be a slower night.

She got in the parking lot and slammed the car door. The lack of secondhand smoke from the outside of the building was a good sign it was dead. She walked in to only a few tables, and no one she was avoiding was behind the bar.

She walked to the back. Kale's door was opened slightly.

"Can I use your computer?"

Kale turned around wide-eyed. "Sit, now."

Farah sat.

"What the hell is going on with you?"

51

She tried to find the words, her eyes filled with tears. Nothing would be able to describe what happened.

"Jesus Christ, Farah." Kale flew up from his seat, hugging her.

"I came to quit. I just don't have a printer for my notice."

"Sleep on it."

Farah wiped her face. Standing up, she walked out. Still no one she didn't want to see was working. She pulled up a seat, ordering the strongest drink she could think of. One of her coworkers slid a martini across the bar, not saying a word to her.

She slammed back the first one faster then she should have. Without anyone arguing, she got a second one. The burning in her stomach from not eating started to consume her.

Penny's voice shouted behind the bar, calling something to someone. Farah was so out of tune about anything until she heard her high-pitch squeal.

"I'm just finishing my drink, then I'll leave." Farah still sat at the bar with her hood over her head. She was surprised she was able to talk without slurring her words.

"You never called me. I was a little bit upset."

The last thing Farah needed was Brett.

Farah covered her eyes with her hands. "Go away. Just stop."

"Johannsson gets to take you for a test drive and I don't? Ouch."

Farah groaned, pulling her hands away from her face, looking at her martini. She picked it up, taking a big drink. She looked down the bar.

Lucas, Brooke, and Penny have gathered on the other side of the bar. Farah slouched, resting her head in her arm.

Farah couldn't feel Brett standing next to her anymore. She raised her head, taking another sip. The room began to spin. She grabbed on to the bar, taking a deep breath. Farah tried to push her drink away but missed it, pushing away air. She blinked, trying to see straight, but everything was duplicated.

"You don't look good." Brett put his hand on Farah's back.

She tried to push him away, but her mind wouldn't make the connection with her arm. "What did you put in my drink?"

After multiple attempts, she successfully was able to rest her elbows on the bar, holding her head.

"Farah, what's wrong?" Penny leaned in the bar.

"Dump the drink," Farah said, low.

Penny was able to hear her. "Lucas, call Thomas now."

"Don't. He doesn't care. None of you do."

"Let's get you home." Brett got close to Farah.

She tried to shake her head no.

Farah could hear blurred chatter around her; but she was stuck, frozen in time, with the sound of her racing heartbeat pounding in her ears.

*****

"What happened?" Farah mumbled, not expecting anyone to answer.

The last thing she remembered was sitting at Off the Strip telling Penny she wouldn't be there long. She squinted her eyes, the bright lights making her headache worse. She rolled over picking up a black hoodie off the floor, pulling it on over her head. She sat on the bed, trying to remember how she got home.

With a sigh, she stood up. The bedroom door creaked as she opened it. Farah groaned in reaction to the loud noise. She dragged her feet to the kitchen, opening the cupboard to get Advil. She turned on the tap, filling up a cup. She popped the pills, taking a sip of water.

She turned around to see Penny, Lucas, and Brooke staring at her. Thomas was sitting with his hands covering his face, his knuckles cut up.

"I'm fine. You can go," Farah said, trying not to sound upset.

"No." Thomas pulled his hands away from his face. He stood up. Before Farah was able to register, he was standing inches away from her. "They were my sisters."

Farah held her head. "How was I supposed to know? You never told me anything. Not like it matters now." Farah stormed away to the bedroom before she started crying, making the headache worse.

Thomas grabbed her hand.

She looked up at him. "What happened to your hand?"

Thomas slipped off his shirt and pants, then shut the bedroom door behind him, crawling under the covers.

Farah sighed. "I didn't say you could stay." She took off her sweater, putting her hand on her stomach. The feeling of hunger was too painful. She opened her eyes, crawling under the covers.

Thomas grabbed her arm. "I was going to wait until you woke up. When was the last time you ate?"

Farah paused. "I can't remember. Tuesday. Wait, Monday, I think."

Thomas looked at Farah. He got out of bed, storming into the living room in his boxers. He started shouting. Farah covered her ears with the pillow. His words cut her mind like glass. She folded the pillow around her head, blocking out some of the noise.

The bed sunk. Thomas put his lips to Farah's. She grabbed a handful of his shirt, scared to let go.

"Brooke was supposed to be staying here. Penny came back for change of clothes, but it didn't look like you were home." He pulled away, resting his forehead on hers.

"I was in bed." Nothing seemed worse to Farah than having to talk.

"For two days?"

Farah bit her bottom lip, trying to deflect the question on him. "What happened to your hand?"

"I saw Brett trying to take you away. You couldn't even talk. I lost control. I have a meeting with the dean and coach Monday."

Farah pulled her eyebrows in, more confused than ever. "What happened last night?"

Thomas explained everything without breathing. He never stopped thinking about it. He looked as tired as she did.

Farah rolled over, completely exhausted and overwhelmed. "I need to sleep. Please go."

"I'm not leaving until you're my girlfriend. We are going to talk about it when you wake up. I love you."

Farah rolled back over. A tear slid down her cheek, landing on the pillow. "I love you."

Thomas wrapped his arm around her shoulder, bringing her body into him as close as she could. Farah took a deep breath. Her eyes got heavy, and she fell asleep.

She woke up in the same position she fell asleep in. Thomas was running his fingertips over her back. The smell of food crept into the room. Farah instantly felt irritated from hunger. She pushed herself from Thomas. She dangled her feet over the edge of the bed, slipping the hoodie over her. He stood in front of her with his arms out. She took his hand, expecting to drop it. He held on to it tightly, leading her out of the bedroom.

The smell only became more intense the closer she got to the kitchen. She stopped around the corner, watching Penny, Lucas, and Brooke cooking her food.

Penny dropped the flipper on the stove. She run up to Farah, wrapping her arms around her. "I'm sorry. I didn't think you where home. You weren't that bad when Ace died. I had no idea."

Farah put her arms around her. That only made Penny squeeze her harder. "Only because Kai was with me."

Lucas joined in the hug. "We both remembered you liked it when we cooked for you."

Farah felt angry at them this morning. She wanted to scream at all of them. Everything she felt before has been replaced. They both knew she wasn't going to snap back for a few days, if not a few weeks.

"You're not quitting now, are you?" Brooked asked.

"No. You can go though."

"Um, why?"

"You moved. Penny stayed."

Farah wandered over to the stove, scooping up her vegetables. She put a spoon in the hummus, taking out a big scoop. The sound of the door slamming put a small smile on her face. She looked up, seeing no one was bothered about Brooke's exit.

She kept catching herself glancing down at Thomas's knuckles. Every time her eyes met them, she would feel herself feeling guilty and responsible for whatever will happen with his future in basketball.

Thomas looked at her. His face sunk, seeing her eyes his hands. Farah felt him wrap her up in his arms. "I was tired of it anyways."

Lucas took the plate from her, walking to the couch. Penny already turned the television on. The first episode of *Friends* was playing.

Farah looked up at Thomas, pulling herself away. "All of this is my fault."

"No, it's not. Come, sit down."

She led the way to the couch. Lucas and Penny began talking about something else. Farah was thankful for any distraction. She put the last pepper in her mouth and dropped the tray on the table. She rested her head on Thomas. Being able to touch him again, being in the same room as her friends again was what she needed all week.

Chapter 8

The first day Farah went back to work had to be the slowest Sunday ever. She was nowhere prepared mentally, but if the last time she felt like this taught her how to feel like herself again, she had to push hard to be herself.

Kai had been sitting at the bar sipping on his warm Budweiser for an hour. Farah leaned in the bar, trying to not feel guilty about him wasting his time being at home.

"Don't spend your time babysitting me."

Kai looked up at her, raising one eyebrow. "I'm not babysitting you. I'm just sitting here waiting for your boyfriend so I can have a chat with him."

Farah laughed until she realized he was serious. "Don't go back, Kai, please."

"Me and Brae were talking about you standing up to Mom and Dad. We are both their robots."

"You're quitting!"

"It's not exactly quitting. Our contracts are up in a month."

Farah put her knee up on the shelf behind the bar. She pushed herself over the bar. She landed on her feet hard, ignoring the pain radiating through her ankle.

Kai laughed wrapped his arms around her. Farah knew that this was going to turn into a full Whitmore war. None of that mattered.

Farah pulled away. Thomas walked past her, kissing her on the cheek, before taking a seat at the bar.

"Thomas, time for a chat." Kai sat up straight. He was trying to look intimidating, but failed when he had to fight back a smile.

"Shit," Thomas murmured.

"Farah, go away."

Farah went to the cooler, stocking up the limited number of beer that was sold to get ready for closing. She grabbed the counting sheet, dreading every minute of it.

She walked back out and wiped the bar again. Kai waved good-bye, then left.

"Ready?" Thomas walked behind the bar, taking her hand to lead her outside.

"You don't have to take me to and from work."

"I'm also spending the night."

Farah cringed. Everyone was babysitting her.

"I missed you."

That was an answer she found herself satisfied with.

She locked the bar behind her. "What did he say to you?"

Thomas shrugged. "Nothing I wouldn't say to protect my sisters. Other than that, he made it very clear that he is trained in shooting."

Farah opened the passenger door, slouching into the seat. "Imagine what it would be like with Ace here."

"I would have been able to handle him too."

Thomas parked on the street. He opened his door and ran around the car. Farah looked up with her purse in her hand, smiling. She grabbed his hand, dragging him in the building.

He pushed the elevator button. When it opened, Farah walked in behind Thomas. She melted into his body. Being able to touch him whenever she wanted gave her a feeling of security rushing through her veins.

The elevator light up the number 6. She groaned when it opened, not wanting the moment to pass. Spices floated in the air. Her stomach started growling, hoping it was coming from her apartment. Farah pulled Thomas down the hall hand in hand.

She opened the apartment door. The smell was coming from her kitchen.

Lucas looked up from a take-out tray, making a disgusted face. "We got you some weird tofu shit." Lucas walked up to Farah and put his arm around her waist. "I love you."

Farah leaned into his arm, closing her eyes tight.

*****

The next morning Farah woke up to the sound of Thomas lightly breathing. The light from the sun rising was poking through the edge of the dark-purple black-out curtains. She reached her hand over, touching his shoulder, dreading his meeting today. If he got kicked out, she had no idea how he was going to pay for the rest of his degree.

She felt as if everything was her fault.

Farah pulled the blanket off her, fighting the bad thoughts from her mind. If she let them win, she was just going to hit an all-time low. She stood up and pulled on her fuzzy pink robe. She opened the door, trying to not make its usual creak. She got it opened just enough to squish her petite frame through. Grabbing the handle with her right hand, twisting the knob, she put her palm of her left hand on the door, slowly closing it.

Everyone was still asleep. No one was supposed to be up for another two hours. She went to the kitchen and cleaned up last night's mess. She got out a pan and opened the fridge, pulling out a package of bacon.

She cut it open. Every time her fingers slid over the raw fat, she had to fight the urge to puke.

I'm sorry, little buddy, they're all vultures. She repeated in her head, trying to push down the guilt.

The bacon sizzled in the pan, grease spit on her robe. Every moral she has lived with since she was fourteen was being broken. She needed to do something, anything for Lucas, Penny, and Thomas, even if it was the smallest gesture for her to say she loved them. Farah just wanted everything to go back to normal. She was already tired of everyone thinking every second she was going to snap.

She grabbed the carton of eggs from the fridge along with a bell pepper. She cut up the pepper, tossed it in a pan long enough for it to become soft, then cracked eight eggs, scrambling them, while listening to the coffee pot beep from the automatic timer.

"What smells so good?" Lucas's feet shuffled along the hardwood floors.

Farah looked down at the pan and frowned. "Burnt bacon. Damn it."

Lucas took the pan off the burner. "It's not bad." He turned on the fan for the oven.

Seconds later, the loud buzzing woke Thomas and Penny up.

Lucas put paper towel on a plate, moving the bacon onto of it, patting it down.

Farah grabbed the pan, looking at the pool of grease. She held it up, turning around. "This shit is going to kill all of you. Imagine what your arteries look like."

"Is there coffee?" Penny asked, rubbing her eyes, ignoring Farah's comment.

Farah watched her boyfriend grab four coffee mugs, creamer, and a burner matt. He glanced over at her straight-faced with no emotion.

He sat down in the stool, holding his head in his hands. Farah walked over to him. She wrapped her arms around his middle, holding him. He grabbed her hand.

"I don't regret doing it."

"I know," Farah muffled against his back. "Thank you."

"I just don't want you to see what I did to him."

Farah held him tighter. The smell of bacon started to make her stomach turn. She walked away to get ready.

*****

Farah leaned against the wall with her arms crossed, her fingernails hurt from biting them the entire ride to campus. Basketball players leaned against the walls and sat on chairs waiting for them to lose another player. Every month it seemed like a team lost a player. College sports put a lot of pressure on the athletes. Between working, studying, and trying to have a social life, people couldn't live up to the expectations. The swimmers on the swim team dropped like flies when they realized there was no excitement from the school. Basketball was the same until people starting placing bets.

The door swung open with Thomas stepping out. "Sorry, boys."

In unison, the entire team cursed different swears.

Thomas walked up to Farah, pulling her in by the waist. She rested her head on his chest. "I'm sorry."

"You don't get to apologize to me. I did it."

The door opened again. Thomas held Farah against him tighter. She looked at Brett. She couldn't peel his eyes off him. His entire face was swollen. She didn't have a medical degree, but it looked like Thomas fractured his jaw. Not one, but both of his eyes were purple. His nose had a splint on it. Brett walked by, staring at Farah. Her body stiffened. Thomas turned around, shielding himself between the two of them as he walked by. Farah saw from the corner of her eye that everyone from the team was watching them, ready to split up another fight.

Farah tried not to think about seeing Brett. She expected to feel humiliated, but the only emotion she could feel was hatred.

"Please tell me he's off the team," Lucas said loud enough for everyone to hear, including Brett.

Thomas nodded. He peeled his eyes off the back of Bret's head. Looking down at Farah, he smiled.

Mike stormed past to catch up to his friend. "Nice going, Farah," he muttered as he walked by.

Penny's mouth dropped open. "Unbelievable."

Lucas held on to Penny, giving her a stern look of warning not to say anything else to Brett. "I'll walk you to bio."

"I'll catch up." Farah grabbed Thomas's hand, leading him outside.

Thomas opened the door, stepping outside. He grabbed Farah, pulling her in close, warding off the chilly weather. He slid his hands down her back and into her jean pockets. "What's on your mind?"

"How are you going to pay for school?"

"I have a bit of money in my college savings account. I called my mom. She said there is enough in there to cover this semester and next year. By the way, everyone's dying to meet the girl I threw my scholarship out for."

"No pressure," Farah mumbled. "There are six of you?"

Thomas lowered his eyebrows. "You really don't know much about me. Go to class. I'll fill you in over the next sixty or so years."

He pulled his hands out of her jean pockets. Farah watched him jog across the lawn to a group walking in to the language building. A redhead in the group stopped to wait for him. She looked past Thomas to Farah and smiled. Thomas turned around to Farah. He gave her a wink before walking away. Everything was in his past, and he has done everything to prove to Farah that he really does love her. Two weeks before, she would have felt the worst kind of jealousy burning in her chest; all she could feel was contentment.

Farah sat next to Penny in the biology lab. She still wore the same smile on her face from Thomas talking about the future together.

"Miss Whitmore." Mrs. Delaney stood at the other side of the table sliding a paper across. "We are doing a dissection today. Write me a paper. Hand it in at the end of class."

Farah sighed. She watched Penny tap her fingers. Science was the only thing Penny couldn't wrap her head around, other than Shakespeare. Bio never had numbers, so it came natural to Farah. Farah shook her head, preparing herself to break another moral in less than four hours. "I need to help Penny with this. I'll stay."

Penny hugged Farah. "I love you."

"You better, first bacon now this bullfrog."

The teacher's assistant set the frog on the table.

Farah had to turn her head from throwing up. "I hate you," she said, covering her mouth. Farah looked down at the greenish-gray dead reptile. "Sorry, buddy." She leaned back in her seat, cursing herself for staying in class. Knowing that this frog was taken from its home in the wild and pumped with chemicals to keep its body from decaying just to educate students. Farah looked around the classroom, disgusted that this isn't the only class in the country that did this.

Penny picked up the knife. She placed it on the bullfrog.

Farah let out a gag, covering her mouth. "I can't do this." She grabbed her purse and ran out of the classroom, fighting for the eggs and coffee not to come up.

She put her for arm against the wall, resting her head into it, trying to breathe. Farah zoned out. After a while, she felt the blood rush from her head back into her heart. The smell of Penny's perfume circulated around her. She knew she was out of class. Farah turned about around, still white in the face. Even after an hour, she still felt sick.

"I got you the paper. Hand it in by tomorrow." Penny tried to sound cheerful.

"I feel so sick."

Farah was taken aback by Penny's laughter.

"You're the best friend anyone could ask for, you know that?"

Farah linked elbows with her. "Have you talked to Brooke? I haven't apologized for kicking her out."

"Don't. She was a bitch anyways. It only got worse when you ended up with Thomas. It just happened behind your back."

"Did you stick up for me, at least?"

"Every single time. Lucas lost it a few times. If she was around, Thomas wasn't."

"Thanks."

"Anything for my fairy."

*****

"O think'st though shall ever meet again?" Farah leaned into the bar, staring at Penny.

"I doubt if not; and all these woes shall serve. For sweet discourses in our time to come," Thomas said, walking to Farah, putting his hand on her hips.

Farah kissed him. "You just got so much hotter. I have no idea you knew Shakespeare."

Penny groaned. "Yeah, okay. What the fuck does that mean though?"

"It's about two young kids who love each other, but family politics are keeping them apart. In the end Juliet chose to be with Romeo in death."

"This class makes me drink," Penny mumbled. She picked up her vodka tonic, chugging it back.

Kai stood up from his seat. He looked at Farah, then looked at the door. Farah followed him outside.

Braelynn was standing on the sidewalk next to a cab. Farah's eyes started to cloud up from the tears running down her face. She tried to breathe, but it turned into a gasp. "You can't go back. You just came home. It hasn't even been a week."

Braelynn wiped her face. "I haven't even seen you much, I've been so busy." Braelynn smacked Farah's arm. "Watch your drinks."

Farah wiped her face again. She was sobbing too hard to keep up with the tears. "A few more weeks then you're back? Forever, right?"

Both of them nodded. Braelynn pulled Farah to hug her. With hesitation from both of their bodies, trembling Kai pulled Braelynn off so he could hug Farah. They both squeezed each other tight.

Kai dropped his hands. He pulled away, his eyes starting to tear up. "We will come back."

Farah took one last look at them before they got into the cab. Her hands trembled. She turned around, opening the door to the bar.

She walked to the bar, not taking her eyes off the floor. Attempting to dry her face, the sleeves of her shirt were soaked. Farah grabbed her purse. She heard Penny shut her textbooks and open her backpack.

"Go with her. I can cover you," Kale said to Thomas.

Farah let out on laugh. "I don't even know why I'm crying this hard. I should be used to them going."

"They'll be back soon." Penny reached for Farah's hand.

*****

The rest of the night the three of them sat at the apartment studying, eating, and laughing. As much as Farah wanted to crawl into bed until they got home, she knew she couldn't let them down like that.

Growing up, the three of them where always at their throats. Ace was the peacekeeper. A few years before he died, they all started to get along, spending almost every free minute together until Ace was recruited. The same month, Braelynn was shipped off to a boarding school. Her dad never said why, just that it was for problem girls and she will come back fixed. That was the same month they moved to Vegas, and Farah didn't remember her sister ever getting into trouble. Every single day Kai was in a room with closed doors fighting with their father about Braelynn. Kai would slam the doors behind him. Once in a while he would phone Ace and update him on their sister. He never cared about only giving good news; Ace was fighting for her as well.

Four years later and Farah still had no idea what was going on. She wanted to ask them every single day, but she was scared she would hate her parents even more.

Chapter 9

Farah opened the bedroom door. Penny's voice echoed through the apartment.

"Are you moving in now or what?"

Farah knew Thomas smiled. "I like spending time with my girlfriend, sue me."

"Just wait until after you both graduate to propose."

"Penny, shut the fuck up. She's going to hear you," Thomas snarled.

Farah stood in the doorway of her bedroom with her mouth opened. It felt like she swallowed her tongue. They haven't even been dating for a month, and he has been talking about marrying her. When he brought their future up, she thought it was just him talking possibilities, not him actually setting a plan in stone.

Shit.

Farah swallowed hard, trying to shake it off.

"What are we doing this weekend?" Farah shouted from the doorway, trying to pretend like she never heard anything.

Out of nowhere Thomas appeared in the doorway. He put his hands on Farah's waist. Even with her hair not brushed and under her bottom lashes were the residue left from yesterday's eye makeup, she melted from the way he looked at her.

She covered her hands with his. She took a step backward. Thomas followed her. Farah kicked the door closed. Moving her hands from his, she snapped the button of his jeans. Thomas looked down at her with a delish grin. He grabbed the bottom of her baggy shirt, pulling it over her head. Farah pulled her panties down to the floor. As she stepped out of them, she gave his shirt a tug.

Thomas pushed her down to the bed. Farah fell back onto the mattress. Her heart was beating out of her chest. She felt even more excited than the first time. She used her elbows to sit up so she could watch him undress. His muscles flexed with every movement.

Thomas put his forehead on hers, positioning himself on top of her. He kissed her slowly, pushing her back down.

Thomas ran his hand over Farah's pink skin. She started breathing deeper. Thomas had his lips in a smile against hers. Farah's heart nearly stopped knowing that he was ready.

"Oh my god," Farah moaned, feeling him inside her was better than she remembered.

Thomas never worried about going slow. He thrust hard against her. Farah grew weak in the legs. She let out a moan.

"Get on your knees," Thomas panted.

Farah rolled over. She rested her cheek against the sheets. She felt his hands feeling her ass. He thrust against her so hard the headboard began to hit the wall.

The more she started to moan, the faster he went. Farah grabbed the blanket with her hands. She arched her back, letting out a loud moan.

"Fuck," he moaned as his body shook.

Farah rolled over to sit on her knees. She watched Thomas wipe the sweat off his forehead. She leaned up, wrapping him in her arms.

He nuzzled his face in her neck. "I'm a bit out of practice."

Farah giggled as she pulled away. With no apology in her voice, she replied, "That would be my fault."

Thomas nodded.

"You have sixty or so years to make up for it."

Thomas grinned.

Farah started to get dressed, her mind was wondering off, thinking about what she heard Penny say. Was she serious? Was that his plan? Isn't twenty-two a bit young to be thinking about getting married?

Farah was brought out of her thoughts to Thomas talking. "Shit. Sorry. I, uhh, I got distracted. Yes, by my girlfriend. Asshole, I'll leave now."

Farah slid on her shirt, trying not to laugh. "What was that?"

"My brother. I have to pick him up at the airport." Thomas eyes traveled to the bed. "I don't know the protocol about leaving after sex when dating."

Farah shrugged her shoulders. "Just kiss me."

Thomas pulled her arm, bringing her close to his body. He wrapped his arms around her, squeezing. "I love you." He put his lips to hers.

Farah's body became weak. She wanted him again. "I love you."

The door opened and then shut behind him. Farah looked in the mirror and grabbed the brush, trying to get the knotted-up sex hair lose. She glanced down at her phone, pushing the home button. It was fourteen hundred hours. She sighed. Sleeping through the day wasn't what she wanted to do.

She walked out to the freezer, pulling out a bag of frozen mangoes, dumping them into a bowl.

"You need to pull your bed into the middle of the room." Penny laughed.

"I heard you earlier."

"What?"

"You telling him to wait to propose till we got out of school?"

Penny's shocked look showed all the screaming she was holding in. "The first minute he laid eyes on you he knew you were the one."

"How do you know this?"

Penny grabbed a fork, stabbing it into the rock-hard mango. "Because I'm not the one he loved in secret."

"Then why did he sleep with you and Brooke?"

"That was my fault. I may have sent him a picture that wasn't for his eyes, then it happened a few days later. You know Brooke. She had to try because I did. Is it weird how you haven't slapped me yet?"

"Very." Farah laughed.

Penny was working her bullshit detector. She squinted her honey-brown eyes. The fork made a tinging noise when it hit the counter. "Oh. My. God. You are only asking me this because you'd say yes."

Farah put her hands out behind her, leaning into the counter. "It's crazy, right? We haven't even had a date. Way too young to even be thinking about it."

"I'm pretty sure it was brought up with Kai. Kai was way too relaxed before he left. Normally, he's tense."

Farah groaned. She is going to have a lengthy talk with her brother before he comes back home. Even with her saying she would say yes out loud, it never felt wrong. Nothing in her life has been a compulsive decision. Everything has been planned accordingly, even the time she was to make her bed was scheduled. She was given no longer than twenty minutes to get ready in the morning. Having a strict military parents who prepared them since the day they were born made for a very tense house.

This spontaneous, life-altering decision was what she needed.

"Yes. I would say yes."

Chapter 10

Thomas parked his car outside his parents' place. Farah tipped her head back against the headrest, trying to breathe. Since the plans were dumped on her last night, she had to scramble to get coverage for her shift.

What if they don't like me?

"Babe, you are making me nervous. Stop it." Thomas reached over the middle console, squeezing Farah's leg.

"Let's go in." Farah unclipped her seat belt. Her stomach was turning so much she felt nauseous.

Farah stepped outside the car, shutting the door. The neighborhood was on the side of the city that wasn't exactly safe. The house had chain-link fence dividing the property. The drive way had two entrances: one was leading up to the one-car garage, the other entrance connected to a driveway that cut across the lawn. The siding looked like it was thirty years newer than the house. The white was blinding against the sun.

Thomas opened the door. The feeling of the unsafe neighborhood was left outside. The house had brand-new flooring, white walls, family pictures hung on the walls. She noticed a few pictures taken off, leaving the screw in the dry wall. They took one every single year together. Farah moved her head to the right looking at the sectional. Two of the brothers looked at Farah with their mouths opened.

Thomas pulled her into his side. "Don't even think about it, dickheads."

Farah laughed once. She never saw him this relaxed before. "Take it as a compliment, baby."

Thomas looked down at Farah with his eyes beaming. It wasn't until that moment she never called him anything other than his name.

One of the brothers stood up. He was taller than Thomas. He had the same brown-colored hair with dark-brown eyes. Brown hair and brown eyes never stood out to Farah, but he was captivating just like Thomas was. "You're the reason he forgot me at the airport." He crossed his arms. Farah braced herself to be intimidated. "I'm Nick."

Farah smiled.

Nick turned around, pointing to the other brother who still hasn't pealed his eyes from Farah. "That's Jacob."

Jacob blinked, breaking his stare. He had dirty-blond hair with green eyes.

Before Farah was able to say anything to them, Thomas grabbed her hand, dragging her down the hallway. The kitchen wasn't as updated as the rest of the house. The cupboards looked old fashion. It only felt homier to her.

"Holy shit, Fucktard actually brought a girl home." She was the same blonde that Farah accused Thomas of sleeping with.

"Stacy, enough." Thomas's mother scolded his sister. She had salt-and-pepper hair. She looked older than what she was. The wrinkles around her eyes only became more defined when she smiled, trying to not be amused by the jab to Thomas.

The second blonde girl popped her head around Stacy. Her blue eyes cut through Farah like Penny's would. "She's gorgeous."

The front door opened. A little girl came charging into the kitchen. Thomas dropped his hand from Farah's. The girl's face lit up when she saw him.

"Uncle!" she shouted as Thomas scooped her up.

Thomas's dad walked around the corner, messing up the girl's hair. Her laughter shot through the house. Farah suddenly felt her mood improve. Farah stood, staring at her, trying to blink. Looking at her was like looking at the photo albums at home. She had hers and Ace's eyes.

Farah shook her head. She's been missing him so much, she will try to find anything for her to hold on to him.

Farah smiled. "Who's is she?"

Thomas set her on the ground. "My oldest brother's."

"Holy shit! You actually took a break from the Bulls to come home," a voice shouted in the living room.

Farah looked at Thomas. She gave him a gentle shove. "Our boss is your brother?"

"Kale knew I loved you, thought it would help me out a bit."

"I just threw up a little," Stacy said with a smile that stretched from ear to ear.

Everyone started to grab dishes, bringing it out to the table. Farah scanned the dishes, seeing chicken, pasta, and salads. She wasn't expecting there to be any food for her to eat. She was used to the meals when she was growing up when her parents would "forget" about her.

"Farah, come here," Thomas's mom called as she opened the fridge. "I made you a personal vegetarian lasagna. I had no idea what to cook you."

Farah stared at her wide-eyed.

"Is that okay?"

Farah nodded, her head trying not to cry. This was a gesture her parents couldn't even figure out for eight years. "You really didn't have to do that for me."

"I'll heat it up for you. Go sit down."

"I can do it."

Farah took the pan from her. She preheated the oven and set it on the rack, waiting for it to heat up. Thomas walked behind her, wrapping his arms around her waist. If this was what they had held for their future, she wanted it. She needed it; she needed him.

They weren't too young to know they wanted to spend their life together. Thomas rested his cheek on Farah's shoulder, kissing her cheek. Farah thought about Romeo and Juliet. They were only thirteen. Other than it being written in the 1500s, they still knew they belonged together, even if it was tragic.

"Settle down newlyweds. You can be apart for a few minutes."

Thomas's body stiffened at Kale's comment.

Farah giggled. She held on to Thomas's hand. The idea of them having forever together started to sound better and better. He ran his hand over her back as he walked away to the dining room.

Farah leaned into the counter as the other siblings came back into the kitchen, grabbing everything that they needed to set the table. She stared at the floor, wishing that her family was more put together. The love in this house was overwhelming; it made her head spin.

After what felt like a century, Farah grabbed the oven mitts from the top of the counter and grabbed the pan from the oven. The cheese on top was boiling. She scooped it on the plate, then walked out to the living dining room.

So many conversations were bouncing back and forth, Farah had no chance in trying to keep up.

"Your last name is Whitmore, right?" Thomas's dad looked up at Farah.

The entire table was silent, listening.

Farah nodded.

Stacy stared at Kale. "It's just that—"

Kale cut her off before she could talk. "It's nothing. Drop it, Stace."

"Emily has her eyes, Kale."

"I said drop it."

Farah bounced her eyes between everyone in the room. They were all trying to hide something.

Thomas grabbed Farah's hand. "Just stop. Braelynn isn't related to Farah."

Farah looked right ahead at Kale. She felt the blood rush from her face. Farah moved her eyes to Emily, watching her shove pasta in her mouth.

Farah slowly shook her head. She couldn't look at anyone. Her skin started crawling. She was stuck between feeling defeated and feeling humiliated. The fights between closed doors all started to make sense to her.

"Those are Ace's eyes." She looked back up at Kale, struggling to look him in the eyes. "You kept my niece from me?"

Kale tossed his fork on the table, pulling his phone out from his pocket. "Yeah, she knows." Kale put his elbow on the table.

"Damn it," Braelynn's voice echoed in the speakers. "Let me see her."

Kale slid the phone across the table. Farah caught it in her hand.

Farah looked up at Thomas. "You could have just told me, then I could have avoided Thomas and not fall in love with my niece's uncle."

Braelynn pushed out a laugh. "Shut up. You guys aren't even related."

"It's still weird." Thomas stood up, walking away.

"You went to boarding school was because you were pregnant. You missed our brother's funeral because they were hiding you."

"I went back to Montana. Three weeks until we can talk about this, okay?"

"I'm pissed." Farah slid the phone across the table.

Farah looked at the table at everyone. She forgot she was around his entire family. At least the dinner hit a level of tense that she was used too.

"Baby, I don't think she's mad at you. I love you." Kale gazed into the phone.

Braelynn sighed. "I love all you guys! See you soon."

Everyone in the house shouted they loved her back, expect for Farah.

Farah slouched in her chair. Her relationship just became awkward. If Braelynn and Kale break up, that would put pressure on Thomas and Farah to break up? Farah covered her face with her hands. She knew her sister well enough that she wouldn't expect Farah to end things with Thomas, but would the brothers be pressured? Farah moved her hand to her hair, taking a deep breath, trying to stop her thoughts from consuming her.

Thomas leaned against the wall in the dining room with his arms crossed. "What now?"

Farah looked up at him, fighting back tears. "I can't lose you again." A tear escaped her eyes. She quickly brushed it away. "Oh my god, you guys, I'm sorry."

Nick smiled. "Any more sisters?"

Thomas smacked him across the head. He walked along the table, sitting back next to Farah. He leaned in to her ear. Instead of saying anything, he pulled away to kiss her on her cheek.

The rest of the night everyone tried not think or talk about what happened at dinner. Thomas kept touching Farah. If she got up, he would watch her. Farah couldn't shake the feeling that he was trying to enjoy the time with her that he had. To Farah, it felt like he was getting ready to say good-bye to her.

The end of the night came along. She hugged everyone before walking out the front door hand in hand with her boyfriend. During the car ride, neither one of them said a word. The music was playing so low that she could hardly hear it. The worry inside of her started to build up. Thomas was acting like that was his way of having a good last night together. Farah was so focused on not to cry. She was fidgeting with the zipper on her hoodie so much she never even saw the apartment come into her sight.

Her lips parted enough to let out a sob. "No wonder I was kicked out of my parents' house when Brae said your last name."

Thomas held onto his steering wheel. "We can't do this. If something happens between us, it's going to cause so many issues for their family."

Farah had tears running down her face. "Then we won't let anything happen to us."

He hit the steering wheel with his palm. Farah jumped at the tone of voice he used. "Why the fuck would they encourage us."

"Because we love each other."

Farah wasn't even sure if Thomas heard her. She wanted to fight for him. The words just weren't coming to her.

"They wouldn't have encouraged us if they knew it wouldn't work out."

Thomas sighed. "Damn it." He laughed. "You heard Penny yesterday."

"What are you talking about?"

Thomas stared at Farah. Her heart was fluttering. "You were too calm at Kale's comment tonight."

"I'm not letting you end this."

"Good."

Chapter 11

Farah slammed her car door irritated. The parking lot was only getting harder to find a half- decent spot. Penny groaned, both of them dreading the walk. The sun was beaming down. It was 10:00 a.m., and it was already starting to warm up. Penny's heels clicked against the hot pavement; Farah could tell Penny was eager to have her boyfriend back. All weekend she had to hear about how annoying basketball practice was.

"Shit! Farah!" Penny screeched.

Farah dropped her textbooks and notebooks on the ground. Two police officers walked up to Thomas. One stood behind him, putting his hands in cuffs. Without thinking, Farah ran up to him as fast as she could. She was panicking; her legs couldn't move as fast as she wanted them too. Everyone who was on campus stopped to watch, Farah's sobbing only drew more attention to them.

"Thomas!" Farah screamed.

She finally reached him, wrapped her arms around him. Fear struck in his eyes. She needed to do something, anything to fix this.

"Fucking Brett," he said in a low tone.

"I'm going to get you out of this."

"Farah, no. The only thing he would want is you, no."

"It's better than you being away from me for the next five years."

Thomas stared at Farah. His eyes reflected his broken heart. She leaned in, kissing him. He stepped in closer, kissing her with everything he could. She put her arms between his, pulling him in closer, holding him one last time.

"I'll call Kale."

"Miss, move," the police officer said, clearly running out of patience.

Farah leaned in again, kissing Thomas. They were separated when his body was pulled to the side. The smell of his cologne lingered in the air. She turned around. Thomas gazed at her through the window. The lights flickered on the police cruiser before it drove away.

Farah put her hands to her mouth, gasping for air. Her chest felt like it was being ripped into pieces. She had to fix this.

She spun around, seeing a few of Thomas's old teammates standing with their mouths opened.

"Where the fuck is Brett!" Farah screamed.

"Cafeteria," one responded, but the furry inside Farah made her not care which one.

"Tell Penny she needs to call Kale."

She watched them all nod before she ran off.

She opened the cafeteria doors, panting. Brett was standing by a garbage can talking to Mike. Both of them looked impressed with themselves. That pissed Farah off even more.

She ran up to Brett, slamming the sides of her fist into his chest. "You need to drop the fucking charges!" Her voiced echoed. Every set of eyes in the room were drawn to her.

"I can't do that." Brett beamed.

Farah dropped her hands to her side. "I'll do anything." Her voice did a complete 180-degree turn, making her almost completely quiet.

She looked up at Bret. His eyes were still bruised. The healing time in the past week just made them more purple. His jaw was less swollen, and the splint on his nose was gone.

"You're coming to my dorm room then."

Farah almost asked him to repeat what he said. Her mind stopped spinning out of shock. She thought maybe Thomas was being overdramatic. His heartbroken eyes came into her mind. Tears fell down her face.

"Tick-tock."

Farah wanted to punch him. Every time he talked, she hated him more. "Lead the way. You are calling the police station to drop the charges *before* anything happens."

Brett looked at Mike before he escorted her out of the cafeteria.

Farah hugged her arms close to her body. Thomas was going to lose his mind over this. She never cheated on someone before. Even doing it to save his future felt too screwed up. She thought of pushing Brett in front of a moving car. That would only make things worse, and Thomas would still be sitting in an interrogation room.

Brett unlocked the door to the dorms. She walked past a room, not paying any attention to the surroundings. Her heart felt like it was breaking, the guilt already weighing down on her. He stopped, unlocking another door. Farah stood in the messy dorm room.

"Drop the charges on Thomas Johansson. I got what I needed." Brett hung up the phone.

"Give me your phone. I need to make sure it was the police department," Farah said, almost unable to talk.

Bret called it again, putting it on speaker. "Las Vegas Police."

He hung up the phone, and Farah took off her jacket. Before the jacket even hit the ground, Bret walked up to Farah, putting his lips on hers. She cringed; he felt like acid. Her face became soaked with more tears.

"Get out of my room." Brett pulled away.

Farah wiped her face.

"He lost you the second you followed me. Him getting released will be worse than prison. Thinking I fucked his girl is better than actually fucking you."

Farah bent over picking up her jacket. She pulled her phone out of her pocket, sobbing. She slammed the door closed behind her, rushing to the vehicle. The word already spread like a wildfire, what they think happened.

"Where are you? Don't tell me the rumors are true." Penny's heartbroken voice made Farah cry harder.

"I never slept with him. He just wants Thomas to think I did."

Farah ran to the car with her legs shaking. Everything was so screwed up. Them almost breaking up about sharing the same niece seemed like children's play compared to this.

Farah unlocked the car door. The passenger and back seat door opened. She didn't care who came in. She just needed to get to the closest police precinct to fight for her relationship.

"Be ready for him to hate you." Lucas grabbed her shoulder.

Thomas would never be able to hate Farah more then she hated herself.

Driving miles over the speed limit, running yellow lights, they finally got there.

Jacob walked out of the police station. He tried to stop Farah from going in. Through her flailing arms and her kicking her legs, she got free. Inside stood all his family members looking worried and upset.

"Farah, leave. I'm replacing you at work. Stay away from my brother," Kale screamed, looking away from her.

Thomas walked out. He locked eyes with Farah. "I told you not to do it."

"I never slept with him." Her voice was at the point of begging. "You need to believe me."

Thomas shut his eyes, shaking his head.

Farah couldn't think of a single word to try to make any of this better. She got the charges dropped. That was what she wanted. Even if it meant he hated her, it was still better than him being in jail.

Lucas grabbed Farah's arm. Her vision was still locked on where he stood before. She let out a scream mixed with a sob. Her broken heart was worn on her sleeve, but Thomas hated her too much to care.

Chapter 12

Farah felt as if time was being stolen from her. She switched all of her university courses to online to save Thomas the embarrassment of sitting in the same class as her. Between that and getting fired, she hasn't left her apartment in what felt like weeks. Not that Farah knew the difference. When her fridge ran low, she got food delivered or Penny went to the store for her. Studying eighty hours a week was frustrating, even more frustrating when she got lost in her thoughts thinking about when she sat next to Thomas. She spent an hour a week applying at bars around her house. She was more focused on figuring out history and math, knowing she still had two months saved for her to survive on.

How to mend a broken heart was her top search on Google. Every day, multiple times a day, she searched it, hoping a new blog post would show up, giving her any kind of support or ideas to help fix the boulder that sat on her chest.

Farah shoved her textbook beside her, making her notebooks and laptop crash land on the floor. The slightest thing will turn Farah into a weeping mess.

"Fuck everything," Farah said louder then she should have.

"Fairy! We have to go get your last check." Penny stopped to look at Farah. "After you shower. You are disgusting."

"I can't go, Penny. Go for me, please."

"You need to sign for it. He's practically your brother-in-law. I'm sure it won't be bad."

Farah used the couch to stand up, leaving her mess on the floor. She dragged her feet to the bathroom, trying to stall. Last thing she wanted to do today was run into Kale, let alone Thomas. God forbid Lucas will be there, then he'll be stuck in the middle. Lucas and Penny both told her they aren't going to give her updates about Thomas. They also said they haven't been updating Thomas on Farah. She took that as he was asking about her. The look Penny and Lucas shared was the clarity Farah didn't want. He never asked about her; he never thought about her.

Farah undressed, stuck her hand under the running water, listening to the pipes complain. The water turned hot, so she stepped in. Penny was right; the grease from her hair was undeniable. Farah pumped her hand full of shampoo, running her fingers through her hair. Her mind jumped to every single worst-case scenario. The toxic thoughts made her eyes fill up with tears. She turned the water off. Stepping out, she wrapped herself in her hot-pink spa towel. Her wet feet slapped the hardwood floor as she walked across the hall to get to the only bedroom on that side of the apartment.

Farah dropped the towel, put on her orange push-up bra, rushed her hair, and put a black spaghetti strap tank top over her head. Farah never realized how much she was slacking on cleaning. The only pair of underwear she had left was a black thong she bought years ago. It still had the tag on it. She ripped it off before sliding it over her knees.

"Damn it," Farah mumbled, looking down at a pair of short shorts in her dresser.

Farah walked out of her bedroom. Her hair was still dripping down her back. Penny looked at Farah and clicked her tongue before she spun in a half circle, making it look more dramatic with her dirty-blonde hair catching in the air.

Farah looked down. "I haven't done laundry. It's not what you think."

"I know, but Thomas won't." Penny grabbed Farah's car keys from the counter.

Farah ran to catch up to Penny. She was excited to finally see Thomas. She was terrified at the same time. He wouldn't care she walked in. He would probably find the closest girl to him and start hitting on her, just to prove to Farah that he moved on and he doesn't care about her.

Farah made Penny drive. She regretted her decision not to drive halfway there when three cars honked at them. After four years of friendship, she wasn't able to ever recall Penny even being in the driver's side.

Off the Strip looked different. It was the same. The only thing that changed was that it felt unwelcoming to Farah.

"I got my check last night. I just figured you didn't want to come alone," Penny whispered to Farah.

Farah walked in the bar to Kale's office. He looked up at her, tossing her last paycheck on the table. She reached for the pen with a shaky hand. Signing for the last check of a job she loved was the worst thing she could imagine.

She picked up the check and spun around. Taking two steps from the office, Thomas walked up. He looked down at her. She could still see his shattered heart. Correction, that was the worst thing she could imagine.

"I'm leaving." Farah pulled her gaze from his eyes before she broke down in tears.

She walked briskly out of the office. Leaning against the bar was her sister. She was holding a drink chewing on the straw.

"Brea!" Farah ran up to hug her. "When did you get into town?"

"Yesterday. I just went to the apartment. You weren't there."

Farah held up her check.

"I'm getting married tomorrow. I want you to be my maid of honor."

"I wish I could. You know it's not a good idea for me to be there. You also know I don't have money for a dress."

Braelynn stared at Farah. At first, she looked hurt, then she looked severely pissed off. "I didn't realize how selfish you were."

The air was knocked out of Farah's lungs. She hasn't done one thing selfish especially to her sister.

"Back off, Brae." Kai stood behind Farah.

Braelynn covered her face with her hands. "I'm sorry. You don't need to be in it, just come. Even if you're in the back row. Forever Cupid, thirteen hundred hours."

Farah nodded her head, cringing. The thing she wished this family would stop doing is telling time in twenty-four hours.

*****

It took Farah hours to get ready. The only thing she had that was even relevantly a nice dress was a knee-length black fitted dress with a jewel neckline. The wedding chapel was pink with a giant cupid outside. Farah blew the loose piece of hair that hung from her face, haunting her that she forgot to curl it. She stared at the tacky-looking building. After the problems they had in their relationship, Braelynn and Kale probably didn't care where they got married, just as long as they were married.

Someone knocked at Farah's window, making her jump. She took the keys out of the ignition, opening the car door, glaring at Kai. "You scared me."

Kai grabbed her elbow, dragging Farah up the pathway. "Come on, we'll sit in the back."

"No. I'll sit in the back. You sit up front." Farah opened the door of the chapel.

Farah looked around the walls, pictures of newlyweds hung in frames.

"You didn't do it. You and Thomas will work it out."

Farah shook her head. "No, we won't. It's not the fact I didn't do it, it's because I almost did it." Farah grabbed onto Kai's hand. "I can't be here, his entire family. None of them will even make an attempt to believe me."

"If you want to run out on your future wedding, call me, but if I let you run away right now, our sister will murder me."

More people started to gather into the lobby. Despite Farah's new need to run away from everything, she walked into the doors and sat in the back row.

Thomas looked around. His eyes met with Farah's. She turned her head, looking away, wiping under her eyes. She thought he was hot before. The suit he was wearing topped that. He was perfect in every way possible. Sitting in the same room as him for the first time in weeks was harder than she thought it would be.

Music played. Thomas sister walked in. The entire night she spent with his family she wasn't able to figure out her name. Stacy walked behind her. Farah put her elbows on her knees, holding her head.

"Farah, are you okay?"

Farah looked up. "What the hell, Brea. You can't stop walking down the aisle to check up on me." Farah laughed once. It was small enough to convince herself she was okay.

Braelynn rolled her eyes. "Thank you for coming."

"Give me a hug." Farah stood up, wrapping her arms around her, whispering, "If you weren't right about me being selfish, I would be standing with you. I'm sorry."

Farah sat back down, watching her sister walk down the aisle in a white lace dress. She tried to be happy for her. She was happy for her. She finally gets to have the life she had to lie about for years.

Farah couldn't physically handle sitting in the same room with Thomas. The guilt weighed down on her even more. As soon as they had their first kiss as man and wife, Farah stood up, quietly opening the door, trying to be unseen. The main door to the chapel appeared in her line of sight, and she ran outside as fast as she could in the tight dress to her car.

She scrambled, checking her bra for her keys and phone. She was too distracted and left them on the bench. Tears started to fall down her face. She ran to the side of the building, down the straight road. She can across a shrub that was big enough to hide her. She sat down behind it and cried.

Hours passed; her head was pounding. The sun moved across the sky. Her stomach growling was telling her dinner was getting close. She stood up, wiped her face, dusted off her dress, and walked back to the chapel like nothing happened.

The door of the chapel was wide open. "Did someone drop off my phone and keys?"

"Farah?"

"That's me."

The women set down her phone, and the picture of her and Thomas lit up the screen. Farah felt even smaller than she did when she spent the afternoon crying behind a shrub.

*****

Farah walked into the apartment. Lucas cranked his head to look back at her. He stood up from the couch. "I'll get the ice cream."

Farah squinted her eyes at him, then marched into her room. Eyeliner ran all the way down her face. Leaves were caught in her hair. She shut the bedroom door, stripping off her dress. She slipped on a baggy shirt, not paying attention to what it was. She grabbed a pair of sweat pants from the floor. Every curl in her hair fell out, leaving her with waves. The brush never even put up a fight. After she struggled getting the eyeliner from her cheeks, she went into the living room.

Lucas looked at her wide eye. "You might want to change." A knock on the door sounded through the apartment. "Or not."

"Are you ready?" Thomas deep voice sent a sense of comfort through Farah's body. Her home felt like home again.

"I just have to say good-bye to Penny." Lucas backed up.

Thomas groaned in protest. He shut the door and walked into the apartment. Farah froze, seeing him.

Thomas looked at Farah. "Uh, can I have my shirt back?"

Farah looked down. "Oh my god."

She turned around. Her cheeks flared red. She got the T-shirt off her as fast as she could manage. Paying attention, she grabbed a black shirt and slipped it over her head.

Farah opened the door, holding the bunched-up shirt in her hand. She wasn't even aware he had left it there. Giving it back to him felt like a cruel joke. "I never did it." The words slipped out of her mouth. She wasn't able to control the begging.

"I have someone waiting for me. Lucas, hurry up." Thomas had put a wall up. There was no way she was getting through to him.

Farah backed away. She guessed he had moved on. The person standing in the entryway wasn't Thomas. He shielded himself from any kind of feelings.

"Okay, I'm back." Lucas pushed his glasses up on his nose.

"Better not keep whatever *sank* he has today waiting." Farah spit the words out.

Thomas laughed with no humor. "At least I didn't fuck the guy who drugged me."

"I never did it!" Farah screamed.

Penny's door flew open.

"I almost did, to keep you safe."

Farah thought she saw Thomas expression soften out, then he opened the door, slamming it so hard the cups in the cupboard shook.

Farah turned around, walking to her bedroom. She heard Lucas say good-bye to Penny. Farah's body crashed against the mattress. Tears have already begun to soak her pillow. Penny covered her up and pulled Farah into her, holding her.

Chapter 13

Farah spent the next morning at the library making her resume perfect. She knew she needed to move on with her life. A new job, or any job, at all was going to help her.

*****

The sun was starting to heat up the morning air. She should be sitting in on a class right now, but moving on seemed too important. She looked up to see a country bar. She puffed out a breath of air.

As soon as she opened the door, music blared. Either she was going to turn clinically insane or end up loving country music. The first option seamed more practical.

Farah walked up to the bar. The bartender held out her finger, then walked to the back. Farah looked around. The standing-up drink menus on the table said, "Saddle 'Em," in bold baby-blue print.

"Howdy." A man, late thirties-early forties, walked up to Farah.

Oh, dear god. Farah thought.

"Let's see your resume."

Farah handed it over to him.

"Are you in school?"

"I am. I can work after fourteen, sorry, 2:00 p.m." Farah cursed herself.

"Come back today at 2:00 p.m. We will get you a uniform and start training."

Farah nodded. That was too easy. This was going to suck.

Farah shut the door behind her, walking outside in the blinding sun. She had three hours until her first day of work. She stopped in her tracks to see Braelynn and Thomas's sisters holding Emily's hand walking down the sidewalk. Farah stood there feeling hurt in ways she never even knew was possible. This was what Thomas wanted to avoid. It just never crossed her mind that Farah was going to be put second to his family.

Braelynn cackled. "Now I've seen everything."

Farah looked down, shrugging. "Shut it. I needed a job."

"Come on, Rachel, let's go." Stacy picked up Emily, tugging on her sister.

"No." Rachel swatted Stacy away from her.

Farah glanced up at Braelynn, watching her close her eyes and taking a deep breath. She was stuck in the middle of a family that had so much love and one who wasn't even holding together.

"I'm surprised you are even in town. I thought you guys would have gone somewhere." Farah shoved her resumes in her oversized purse.

"We are setting up the dinner. The wedding was sudden. No time to plan anything." Braelynn shut her eyes, regretting the words.

Farah nodded her head, understanding why she wasn't invited.

She looked past her sister, drawing her attention on a family across the street. She may have understood why she wasn't invited, but she never understood any of this.

The only thing Farah wanted to do was be a part of her sister's new life. She gazed off at the three-year-old. Her hair was strawberry-blond hair with natural crazy curls that went every direction. Emily looked up at Farah, smiling, showing off all of her baby teeth. Farah turned away after offering a smile. Farah's heart sunk into her stomach. Her niece had no idea who she was.

Farah started to back away. All of this was too much for her to handle. She was ready to walk away from her parents; her sister was too hard to walk away from. Kai would be on Braelynn's side through everything. They always had each other's backs.

Farah froze, remembering she lived in her sister's apartment. She raised her hand to her head, running her fingers through her hair. Her body was trembling. Even though Farah was trying to breathe through it, she felt the tears burning her eyes.

"Have fun tonight." Farah looked at the ground, trying to hide her pain. "Penny is going to need a bit of time, but I'll be out of your place by tonight."

Farah turned around, pushing the unlock button on her key fob. Her mind was spinning, trying to think of a place to stay. Lucas was out of the question; he lived with Thomas. The only two logical things were the back seat of her car or crawling back to her parents. Farah sped back to the apartment, wondering how her life became so screwed up. She only had a short amount of time to pack and head off to work.

Farah unlocked the apartment door. Both Lucas and Penny were sitting on the couch. She filled them in with everything that happened before running to her bedroom, packing her clothes. She stuffed it all in a suitcase and walked back out to the living room.

"Where are you going to stay?" Lucas asked, already knowing the answer.

"I have to go." Farah diverted his question, not knowing how to answer.

*****

The first night was worse than she thought it would be. After the songs played through the first time, Farah bit her tongue when she caught herself singing along. The drink orders were easy, all beer. It was almost a relief, compared to all the cocktails that were ordered at Off the Strip. No one who went to her university worked there. No one knew what she did, or didn't do. It was a fresh start in the same city. The night was busy. Bartending in at a different bar didn't make a difference in your drink quality if you were trained properly. She got the drinks out faster than they were being ordered. The line up at the bar was half the size than she was used to, making her life easier.

"What's your story?" the bartender asked Farah.

She looked at his frosted tips. He looked like a Backstreet Boy lost in the wrong decade. He waved his hands around when he spoke, only making him look more flamboyant.

"Don't pester the new girl, Will." The manager from earlier in the night stood beside her behind the bar. "Go home, both of you. Good job tonight, kid."

Farah smiled, turning around to leave. She was happy to be leaving, but it hit her like a semi when she didn't know where home was. She walked out to her car that was parked next to the sidewalk. She unlocked it, sliding into the driver's seat. The air cooled down fast in the desert, making the car chilly. Farah set her arms on the steering wheel, trying to think of a plan, but nothing came to her.

Someone knocked on the window. Farah rolled it down, not looking over. "Can you give me a ride home?"

Farah turned her head, looking at Rachel. She knew this was a bad idea. "Get in, just be ready to get shunned."

Rachel opened the passenger side door. "Pass me your phone. I'll put my address in."

Farah picked up her phone, pushing the home screen. The screen stayed black. "It's dead." Farah stared at it, not knowing when it was going to be turned on again.

Rachel pulled hers out. The GPS started talking. "I don't think anyone thanked you for keeping my brother out of jail."

Farah sat in the driver's seat, not saying anything.

The GPS started talking again, saying they reached the address. She never needed a ride. They were a block away.

Rachel grabbed the door handle. "Where are you staying?"

"I'm going to a friend's," Farah said the first thing she could think of.

"Go back home. Your sister didn't want you to leave."

"I didn't either, but if she has to choose between you guys and me, I won't let her pick me."

"Damn it." Rachel opened the door, jumping out she opened the back door before closing the passenger's door. "Either you're coming with me, or I'm robbing you—choice is yours."

Farah's mouth dropped opened. She opened her door, ready to cause a fit. Rachel had already walked to the door. Farah followed her. This was a bad idea, but she was exhausted.

Rachel owned a house. It was small, two bedrooms at the most. Just like her parents' house, the inside was covered with family pictures. A few of them had Braelynn in them. Her sister had a smile that wasn't shown around the Whitemore family. She looked generally happy.

Looking at her smile, Farah felt toxic. No wonder she lost everything.

"There's a charger plugged into the wall down the hall, last door on the left." Rachel shouted from somewhere in the house.

Farah walked right down the hallway. The room was tiny with white walls. The bed had a plain black blanket covering it. Farah plugged her phone in, crawled under the blanket, and fell asleep.

Chapter 14

Farah woke up in panic, not remembering where she was. Her mind settled when she got a whiff of Thomas scent. Farah remembered she was at his sister's house. He was probably the last person in this bed before her. She rolled over, wide-eyed, staring into Thomas's dark-brown eyes.

"Don't hit me," he said quickly. "I just heard you were here. Next thing I knew, I was in bed with you."

"I'm sorry, I'll leave. Don't be mad at you sister." Farah flew up from the bed.

"I'm not."

Farah went to her phone, unplugging it. It was only 7:00 a.m.

"I'm sorry I accused you of cheating on me."

"I didn't give you much to go off of. It was what he wanted."

Farah's eyes were still heavy. Even though she slept all night, her exhaustion weight down on her. Thomas stood leaning against the wall. He was lost for words. Farah collapsed sitting on the bed. She wanted to walk away, but being this close to Thomas felt so right. She wanted to deny it, but she couldn't.

Farah tucked her hair behind her ear. "I wasn't even sure I was supposed to stay here last night."

Thomas fell on his knees in front of Farah. He placed his hands on the outside of her thighs. "I fucked things up pretty bad for you, didn't I?"

Farah wasn't going to argue. She lost her home, her relationship with her sister was barely hanging on, she was fired from her job, even the luxury of going to class was taken away so she could give him more peace.

Farah tapped her foot on the ground, trying to fight back more tears. Every day it felt like all she did was cry.

Farah's body was moving before she could even comprehend what she was about to do. She moved in closer to his face. Her body so close to his that it washed the heartbreak away. She slammed her lips into his. He kissed her with no remorse. Farah wrapped her arms over his shoulders, pulling him into her. She expected him to pull away; he just held her tighter. He was hungry for her. Every flick of his tongue made her realize how much she needed him for the rest of their lives.

Farah pulled away, instantly regretting it. She already missed his lips. "I love you."

She wanted to say so much more. Nothing felt suitable, nothing felt like it would be enough. Thomas stood up. Farah dropped her head disappointed that her last wild attempt failed. Nothing in her life felt worth it if he wasn't hers.

"Stand up." Thomas made a hand motion with his palms facing up.

Farah stood, ready to walk out of the house embarrassed.

Thomas grabbed her hips, placing a small peck on her lips. Farah didn't know what was going to happen; all she knew was that she needed to fight harder for him. She jumped on him, wrapping her arms around his shoulders and legs around his middle.

Farah buried her face in his neck. "Can we do this again? Can I have another chance?"

Thomas wrapped his arms around her. "It's me that's getting another chance here, not you. I should have trusted you. I should have believed in you."

"Thomas, stop. Please stop."

Thomas turned around, opening the bedroom door. He kept walking. Farah stayed attached to him. Her eyes were shut tight, mostly to avoid the awkward looks from anyone who was at the house.

Thomas's chest vibrated as he began talking. "No one talks about what didn't happen. Don't even think about it." Thomas laughed. "I don't mean this in a bad way, but you're getting heavy, babe."

"Shit, sorry." Farah unhooked her arms, running her hands down his chest.

"Your sister gave me these. In case I broke down and begged for you back." Thomas dug his hands in his pockets. He pulled out her apartment keys. "I'll go get your bag."

Farah nodded, turning her head, watching Rachel and Jacob staring at her.

Jacob sat back, putting his feet on the coffee table. "Now we can stop listening to the crybaby bitch."

Thomas came back and grabbed Farah's waist, staring at her but talking to his siblings. "Dinner tomorrow, let everyone know. You guys know the place."

"Yeah?" Jacob raised his eyebrows, making his forehead wrinkle.

"Are you sure?" Rachel glanced at Thomas and Farah.

Thomas gazed into Farah's eyes. "I've never been so sure of anything."

*****

"I'm at least driving you then." Thomas said, eating a mouth full of half unthawed mango.

"I know you missed me. I missed you too. I can't have you sitting around waiting for me to get off on my second day." Farah leaned into the counter.

Farah looked around the apartment. She was the only one who lived there. Penny was refusing to come back. Apparently, living with Lucas was better than living with her.

Farah watched Thomas breathe out cold air while he ate. "Move in with me."

Thomas coughed.

Farah let out a puff of air. It was too soon to ask.

"Me? Move in here. Like in your bed?" Thomas stood up, walking around the island. He put his hands on Farah's hips, making her melt. "I'll pack when you're at work."

Farah wrapped her arms around him, holding him in to her as close as she could. The past few weeks was a roller coaster, but this moment of peace, the feeling of the word falling perfectly on its axis was worth it all.

"I never thought I would see the day where Thomas Johansson would have a domestic relationship."

"You just never paid close enough attention. When do you have to leave for work?"

"Half hour."

Thomas picked Farah up. Her laughter would be heard from a block away. The tears that were shed in this apartment, the pain that she felt since they first started dating was replaced with a feeling of forever.

Chapter 15

The hardest thing about coming from a family that wasn't close was having to adjust to dating someone with a close family. Farah has only been to one family event with Thomas, and the thought of having to go to dinner tonight was making her want to scream.

She tried to get out of it. Thomas spent hours being too persistent about no one shaming her, so she finally gave in. As much as she didn't want to.

Farah parked her car outside a stone-brick restaurant. The sign on the building said "Luigi's" in handwriting. Farah sat back and sighed. Growing up, this was her family's restaurant. She avoided it at all costs since Ace passed away.

Thomas grabbed Farah's hand. "Braelynn was hesitant when she found out this was the place we were going too. I'm sorry. We can go somewhere else."

"No, it's fine. Are you sure your family is going to be okay with me being here?"

"Positive."

Farah got out of the car, straightening the same dress she wore on her sister's wedding. If she was going to be brave enough to show her face, she might as well look good while doing it.

Thomas grabbed her waist, pulling her into him. "They love you. They just didn't want to see me hurt. If it wasn't for you, I would be rotting in a jail cell, worried about you leaving me."

Farah got on her tippy toes to kiss him. She pulled away anxious to get dinner over with.

Thomas opened the door, and her nerves started to bother her. It wasn't because she was scared; it was the memories of her family when they weren't so broken. Thomas grabbed her hand, leading her through tables. The back of the room had square tables pushed together. Farah glanced up to Thomas. He was fighting back a smile. Lucas sat next to Penny. There was an open chair next to her, and Kai sat across from the empty chair.

Farah pulled out the chair. She sat down, trying not to slouch. The looks she was got from his family made her uncomfortable. She reached under the table, grabbing Thomas's hand. He squeezed hers, reassuring her that everything was okay.

Farah cleared her throat right as Lucas slid the basket of bread with plate of balsamic vinegar and olive oil in Farah's direction. Even as an absent friend, he was always there for her to fall back on.

"Fifi," Emily yelled.

Braelynn started laughing. "Our parents cursed us with our names. She can't say Farah."

Farah stared at Emily. She knew who she was.

The farther they got into dinner, everyone eventually started breaking off in their own conversations. By the time dinner came, Farah went through two baskets of bread, completely stuffed. She stared at her dinner, only eating a little of it before boxing it up.

She looked over the dessert menu, already knowing what she was getting. She had no room left in her stomach, but she was going to force herself to eat it. The server walked by. Farah turned around facing her. "Three panna cottas."

Farah turned back around, watching her siblings look at each other. It became a tradition for the four of them to share one every single time they came.

Thomas stood up from the table, rushing over to the server, catching her before she went to the back.

Everyone listened to Thomas's demand. No one in his family looked at Farah with distrust. It was almost like everyone believed her, or they believed in Thomas's instincts to trust him enough to trust Farah.

Thomas sat back down. He was tapping his fingers off the table. His nervous vibe was radiating off him. Farah began to panic. Her heart raced out of her rest.

"What's wrong?" she accidently said loud enough for everyone around her to hear.

Thomas shook his head as the desert was placed in front of her. Farah picked up the spoon hoping that she could eat away anything bad that was flowing through Thomas's mind. She inhaled a big spoon full. Peace washed over her as soon as the panna cotta hit her tongue.

Farah groaned, feeling something hard against the roof of her mouth. She pushed it to the front of her mouth, disgusted. Her tongue fit in the center. She swallowed hard, spitting out the foreign object in her hand.

A ring.

"I thought she was going to swallow it," Penny muffled into her hand.

Farah cranked her head toward Thomas, confused. "Why do I have this?"

Thomas looked at Farah, grabbing the ring and a cloth napkin from the table. "Spend the next sixty or so years with me as my wife?"

Farah looked at the ring in his hand. He cleaned off the cream, showing a silver band with black diamonds. Her eyes traveled to Thomas. Everything was moving so fast. They just got back together; they just moved in together.

"We have spent more time apart than together. I don't think this is a good idea."

"We had to fall apart before we could fall together."

Farah kissed him with everything she had in her. She pulled back, looking into his eyes. She felt complete peace. "Yes."